Also by Francesca Duranti

THE HOUSE ON MOON LAKE

HAPPY ENDING

Random House New York

HAPPY

ENDING

a novel by

FRANCESCA DURANTI

Translated from the Italian by
Annapaola Cancogni

This work was originally published in Italy as *Lieto Fine* in 1987 by RCS
Rizzoli Libri S.p.A., Milano. Copyright © 1987 by RCS Rizzoli Libri S.p.A.,
Milano.
Library of Congress Cataloging-in-Publication Data
Duranti, Francesca.
[Lieto fine. English]
Happy ending / by Francesca Duranti.
p.   cm.
Translation of: Lieto fine.
ISBN 0-394-57548-2
I. Title.
PQ4864.U68L513   1991 853'.914—dc20   90-53143
Manufactured in the United States of America
24689753
First American Edition

Photograph and Book Design by Lilly Langotsky

FOR
GREGORIO AND MADDALENA

HAPPY ENDING

1

Tried phoning you all day. Lavinia arrives tomorrow. Dinner 8:30. Come.

—Violante

WHITE STATIONERY. Clean-cut edges, no fraying. Large letters, traced with a fountain pen. Dark blue ink. Like an idiot, I sniff it. Unscented.

I take note of every detail with the complacency of someone finding everything as expected. Once it would have been different. I would have eagerly delved into that message, taking it apart, analyzing each of its elements, treasuring every one of them.

This until ten, fifteen years ago. And then, I came to understand that things were more complex than I thought. In other words, I realized there was no such a thing as the "right thing"—the right stationery, the right tone of voice, the right clothes. It was not a sudden revelation, I got to it gradually. But when I did, what a joy. I became more self-confident, less defensive. I gave myself a break.

Still do. I put Violante's note down on the desk and, with a thrill of transgression, slip into my purple silk pajamas: so rich, sleek, and luxurious, so far beyond mere garishness. Voluptuously, I stretch out on my monumental bed.

Since the right thing does not exist, why give up the luxury of occasionally yielding to the wrong one?

Once I had complete faith in vicuna overcoats and Mauritian valets; now I smile at my former innocence with paternal indulgence. Of course, I still have both, the overcoat and the valet: the first, sprinkled with naphthalene, is safe in its plastic bag, while the second, having laid out the purple pajamas on the bed—arms and legs spread, like a corpse floating on the pale blue bedspread—will soon usher in a new day by preparing my breakfast tray.

Indeed, even the Arnolfina is not exactly the right thing, which, however, does not prevent me from being delighted with it. My house is an architectural curiosity, an exception to the rural style characteristic of the Lucca plain. Built in white stone—like the Romanesque churches of the city—it started out as a small convent for a few nuns. The parish archives still contain documents concerning this religious community until 1318, when the archbishop forced the sisters to close up shop and return to the city "for reasons of decorum."

Later, the building was turned into a farmhouse, after which one has to rely on hearsay. It is said that one of its owners was the very same Arnolfini whose portrait, painted by Jan van Eyck in 1434, can be seen at the National Gallery in London. It is said that Arnolfini used the building as an olive press driven not, as has always been the custom in Tuscany, by water, but by the wind, like a Dutch mill. It is also rumored that the press never worked, which does not surprise me. When I bought the Arnolfina, I found no fixtures that might have suggested an olive press—no millstone, no press—but the tower was there, and still is. Thirty-four feet tall, its truncated cone looks extravagant, worse, incongruous in this landscape, and yet so attractive. Without vanes—if it ever had any—and with four large windows on the top, facing the four cardinal points, it rather resembles a beacon or an observatory.

My bedroom is right at the top of the tower.

After going to bed, I switched off the light, but could not fall asleep. So, I got up in the dark, and have come to sit on the large swivel chair—the only token of modernity in my entire house—by the window that overlooks Violante Santini's villa, where I have been so imperiously invited to dinner tomorrow evening. The park, laid out in a semicircle as if to hug the base of the hillock on which my Arnolfina rises, basks in the luminous July night: the large plane tree, the majestic curve of the driveway, the rose garden, the maze of hedges, the swimming pool, and the three houses. They are commonly known as Villa Grande, Villa Piccola, and Limonaia. The first, a three-story Renaissance structure, is where Violante lives, while her younger son, Leopoldo, lives with his American wife in the second—inferior in size as well as age, it being a *settecento* villa with an open gallery on the second floor. As for the third, the lemon house, it was renovated over twenty years ago for Violante's older son on the occasion of his wedding with Lavinia, but it was abandoned barely two months later when Filippo died, and the young widow went to live with her mother-in-law for a few years, and then left for Milan. She comes back every summer, but always as Violante's guest, unable as she is to outgrow the endless adolescence which allows her to be taken in, cared for, supported, and fully relieved of any responsibility even though she has a twenty-year-old son and a few silver threads in her blond hair. Seen from the Arnolfina tower, the three houses—large, medium, and small—resemble those of the three bears: Goldilocks is arriving tomorrow.

Right below my window, in the shady niche formed by the juncture of the tower and the façade of the house, the gardenias are in bloom. Eyes closed, I deeply inhale their scent, a magic ritual that immediately takes me back to what I consider the real beginning of my life.

I was only thirteen, but already tall and strong enough not to hang around when a German raid was expected.

I knew all the parks of the villas around Lucca, having visited them on numerous occasions, albeit always by stealth. The one near the church of Saltocchio was my favorite. Because of the war, some of the parks had been neglected and had turned into thorny thickets from which it was impossible to extract anything useful. Others were so well tended—like the Santini park, the very one I now dominate from my tower—that they put me ill at ease when I snuck in to loot them. But the one closest to the city, the Saltocchio park, only partly neglected, was eminently accessible, and full of nature's bounty: a true paradise. Hidden among its ancient trees, I fished for pike in its pond, gathered firewood, mushrooms, chestnuts. There, I discovered the fruit of an exotic tree whose name still escapes me, as I was never to encounter it again in any of my travels. It must have belonged to a very rare and probably now extinct species. Its fruit were green, shiny, oblong, and filled with a creamy pulp that tasted of cosmetics.

I would get there at dawn, hide the bike in a ditch that ran alongside the park, and climb over the wall. I knew that nobody would show up for another hour or two, and that I had the time to gather all the things I needed and pile them up by the gate; after which I would slip them one by one through the bars, climb back up the wall in the opposite direction, get my bike, and load my booty into a large straw bag.

I never left that garden empty-handed, nor did I ever find in it a definitive—or at least lasting—solution to the problem of survival for myself and my mother. I had to go back every day—whether there or elsewhere—trusting in my luck, keeping on the lookout, avoiding dangers. Was that life as it should be? It certainly was life as nobody wants it to be. I believe everybody's aspirations tend toward a definitive accomplishment that does not have to be repeated every day, and in this my hopes are not different from the rest of the world's. But I am also sure of another thing: throughout that entire period, when every morning brought a new struggle and the stakes were life or death, I tasted a few moments of happiness such as I have never again experienced.

The day I heard people talk of a possible surprise attack, I climbed over the park wall around nine in the evening. Far off, I could hear the German trucks rumbling through the countryside. It was very hot: the summer of 1944 was torrid, at least in Tuscany. All the shutters of the villa were closed because of the curfew, but the panes of the five large French windows off the gallery were wide open. As I emerged from the bushes and crossed the lawn, getting closer and closer to the house, I could hear the sound of voices mingled with the melodious tinkling of crystal and silver: supernatural sounds, like those of magical bells, that seemed to have nothing in common with the opaque clatter produced by the crockery at home. I quietly climbed the steps that led to the gallery, and approached one of the shutters where a partially collapsed slat let through a shaft of light.

There were eight people sitting around an oval table: two men, two young girls, and four women. I never knew their names: they came into my life that evening, left their mark, and disappeared.

A very old servant went silently from one to the other, holding out platters, pouring wine. The lady who sat at the head of the table was also ancient, and, in spite of the heat, wore a white fur stole on her shoulders. I thought she might be ill, unless old age, beyond a certain point, was itself an illness. Across from her, at the other end of the table, sat a white-haired, skeletal man, whom I assumed to be her husband. These were the only three characters, all in their advanced eighties, along with the two girls—whom I respectively placed in the first and last year of elementary school—whose ages I could guess: as if at the beginning and at the end of life nature had the upper hand over statistics, and time engraved its signs according to universal laws I knew.

The other man must have also been past his prime to be dining peacefully while the Germans were combing the countryside. And yet, he was so polished and clean-shaven, with his hair slicked back against his skull à la Rudolph Valentino, that he looked like a young man. Among the other three women— all cool and mellow, and apparently forever fixed at the same ideal age—I intuited blood ties that involved gaps of twenty or thirty years.

Protected by the night, I saw without being seen, very close to them and yet totally extraneous to them. It was like being at the theater, with the stage lit in front of my eyes, offered to my appreciation, except that in this case, the characters were real people unaware of my presence.

I delighted in every detail. The young girls' dresses—identical, aqua-colored and full-length, with their white lace-trimmed collars; the braided uniform of the old servant; the crystal chandelier; the women's hair; the four large still lifes on the walls; the peach-colored tablecloth. Their voices—like the sound of the glasses and the silver—were airy and musical.

I was suffused by a joy that affected all my senses; the last one to be aroused was that of olfaction, which suddenly became alert to a paradisal fragrance—as limpid as water and yet as rich as an Oriental perfume—issuing from a large gardenia bush at the other end of the gallery. In the nearly total darkness, the green of its leaves looked black, and its flowers stood out like haloes of immaculate light. Entranced, I watched the meal all the way to its end, and moved only after everybody else had departed, leaving the old servant to clear the table alone. But I did not move from the gallery. I fell asleep on a wicker armchair and woke up at dawn. Assuming that the danger of a raid was by then over, I went back home, not, however, without first having gathered all the gardenias to bring to my mother.

I was an only child, and my father had been reported missing in Russia. We were never actually told that he was dead, but he never came back. I remember him as a meek man, with few resources. The fact that he was missing did not greatly alter our situation: in our case, poverty had been aggravated by war, not by the absence of the head of the family. My mother treated me like some mythical, miraculous child, the product of an immaculate conception, a rain of fire, a fecundating lightning. In her eyes, I was marked by a lucky star, and destined to do great things.

She spoke of what would become of me in a nebulous but inspired manner. Her prophecies were either infinitely vague or minutely detailed, always leaving the middle ground open. She spoke of "your future" as if it were written in capital letters. "You must never stop thinking of YOUR FUTURE, Aldo, not until it is well under way." Or, shuddering at the long shriek of a recalcitrant kitchen drawer, she would say, "This table will be the first thing we throw away the moment you have a position."

I had no inkling as to what radiant future I was destined for until the morning I went back home carrying that bunch of gardenias. She met me in the kitchen, wearing one of my father's jackets over her nightgown, and we sat at the table drinking barley coffee. Between us, the white flowers floated in a bowl of water.

I was telling her what I had seen through the crack in the shutter, and as I spoke, she placed her knotty hand over mine and squeezed it, hard, almost leaning on it with the full weight of her body. She listened to me with a hungry look on her face, as if my lips were about to drop a choice morsel which she was ready to catch before it touched the table.

Thus prodded, I went on talking, not daring to stop for fear of disappointing her. When I no longer knew what to say, I paused, painfully convinced that my awkward tale had failed to re-create for her what my eyes had seen.

My mother drank the last drop of her coffee, then, resting her elbows on the table, raised her cup, and held it midway between her eyes and mine. It was a white earthenware cup with a green rim, the sort of green that seems deliberately chosen to lend an additional touch of squalor to what—whether public or private—is already clearly poor: the painted wainscoting of the seediest taverns, the doors of drafty schoolrooms, the rusty fly nets covering scanty, unsavory victuals. It is the color of indigence, but for a while, immediately after the war, it became oddly fashionable under the name of "penicillin green." It was as if we could not believe we had the right to shun the greenish memory of military trucks and uniforms. And indeed, for a short while, that color strayed away from its natural habitat to find its place among the first "rich" objects to pop up from the rubble: V-necked woolen sweaters, the armchairs and ottomans of tailor shops, and even the first products of the reborn postwar automobile industry.

But on the morning I drank barley coffee with my mother, back in 1944, penicillin green had not yet become a fad and was still—as it is again today—the trademark of poverty.

"Look at this cup," she told me. A triangular chip on its rim tailed off into a thin, dark, diagonal crack. "Look at it carefully, and don't bother to look at anything else. Everything in this house is like this: my shoes, your mattress, the bicycle, the floor, the ceiling, your father's life, mine, yours."

Despite her words, I cast a quick glance around myself, but the awkward proportions of that room—long and narrow, with a long and narrow window poorly centered on its narrowest wall—immediately discouraged me with their ugliness.

My mother put her cup down and extended her fingers in the air like a pianist who is about to tackle a difficult piece. Then, with her hand, she drew a respectful curve a couple of inches above the bowl of gardenias, as if, not daring to touch the flowers, she had to content herself with caressing the perfumed air around them. She skipped the other half of the metaphor and did not say that there were shoes, mattresses, bicycles, ceilings, floors, and lives like gardenias. She sighed.

"I will not rest in peace," she said, "until I see you all dressed in white, behind the counter of a pharmacy." Her eyes already shone with the brilliance of the snowy smock; the glimmer of vials, jars, and bottles; the glow of the shop windows with their Latin inscriptions, in gold letters on mahogany frames.

Something in the depths of my soul wriggled like a fish caught in a net; but it was so far below the surface that I was only aware of a slight undulation.

Beneath the firm determination and fervent will to fulfill my mother's dreams or die in the struggle, something stirred in the darkness. Maybe it was already the suspicion that the voice which had seduced me that night would call me forth to a whiteness, a brilliance, and a fragrance that had nothing to do with surgical gauze, stainless steel bedpans, or the scent of eucalyptol.

I have been sitting in my armchair for a long time, contemplating Violante's garden. I have left the cracked cup and the horrible kitchen of my childhood far behind me. My mother had the time to see me live, and briefly share with me, a life of gardenias. I look around myself in the circular, moonlit room, and feel profoundly satisfied with every object my eyes fall upon.

I like to spoil myself. Whenever I desire something, I make a point of paying double its worth. The extra money I spend is like flowers, clusters of gardenias on my mother's grave.

I turn my eyes back to the quiet, expectant park. Lavinia is arriving tomorrow.

2

"IT IS NOT BECAUSE of *it*," Lavinia repeated.

"It isn't?!"

"No. It is because of the awful vulgarity of the entire situation."

"Right," Sandro answered. "That, and maybe also because of the idiotic way in which I dissipate myself."

Lavinia strangled the receiver. Why had she blundered into that discussion? Why couldn't she learn to be quiet when there was no point in talking? Why didn't she stop falling in love with men like Sandro?

"Because you see, my dear," he said with the composure of someone who is obviously not in pain, "the truth of the matter is that you fly off the handle because of *it*. Why, in your heart of hearts you can't even imagine that I might desire another woman. How could you possibly accept my decision to spend the holidays with her without making a scene?"

It was the sacrosanct truth, but for some reason or other she didn't feel like admitting it. She wanted to tell him that his behavior was immoral and indecent; instead, she said weakly,

"That's not true, you know it . . . all I ask is that you be civil to me, and honest."

Sandro snickered. "Sure. I should have told you that a lady had invited me to sail around the Cyclades with her. Indeed, I should have also added that the lady in question has a very enticing mouth—soft, pink, and rather small—and a sizeable yacht equipped with all the comforts, and tons of polished brass. And, to conclude, I should have also told you that it is my intention—a most reasonable intention if I may say so—to take advantage of both, the small mouth and the large yacht. Lots of kisses and hugs and see you at the end of the summer. I would have been civil and honest, but you would have raised hell all the same."

Lavinia curled onto the couch, pulling her legs up so as to cradle the aching spot at the center of her body. Three suitcases were lined up by the door; she had already called her mother-in-law to inform her that she was going to spend the entire summer with her in Lucca.

It was too late now to change what had already been decided, first by Sandro when he had announced that he was going away with that woman for a month, and then also by her, when she had realized she would not be able to keep him from leaving. So she had called Violante. "I am coming to stay with you." That last scene was perfectly pointless, and would only make her feel worse.

Fortunately she could count on Violante.

"Come whenever you please," she had answered. "Your room is always ready for you."

That's when she came up with the idea. Why not, after all.

"What about letting me reopen the Limonaia? Everything should still be in order."

That idea had never so much as crossed her mind in the last twenty years. When she was in Lucca, she always stayed at her mother-in-law's. Her bedroom windows overlooked the Limonaia, but she did not see it, nor did she ever think of the two months of her marriage and what they had meant to her.

"I would like to spend the summer in my own house," she had told her. She would throw a few parties, her old Tuscan friends would court her. Most of all Aldo . . . Aldo, whom she so stubbornly refused to take seriously, though he had all he needed to deserve her love.

She would have to move the living-room sofa. She seemed to remember that its present location made the room look smaller. It was a beautiful room, square, with two large French windows opening onto the gray stone patio. She would plant flowers in the big terra-cotta pots that had once been used for the lemon trees—she could already see their color: the hottest pink, carnal, flashy, in a fluid profusion of blooms, nothing stiff, only long stems drooping under the weight of their redolent clusters.

It was not a bad idea. Sandro could do what he pleased.

"In that case, good-bye! Go to your whore with the small mouth and the large yacht," she said.

"That is exactly what I intend to do. A big hug, and I promise I will get in touch as soon as I am back. But now I am hanging up."

Lavinia redialed his number knowing that he would not answer. She clasped the receiver to her aching belly and let the unheeded ringing draw her into his apartment: the darkened rooms, the closed shutters predicting a long absence, his things—each of which was, to Lavinia, a secret fetish—obediently in their place. Sandro had extraordinary authority over inanimate objects, not to mention living creatures: so much so that it seemed as if the world around him—his friends, his work, his home, the passing days—spontaneously organized itself so as to protect him against any setback, disappointment, humiliation, trouble, shame—the basic ingredients of her own life, her daily bread. Lavinia clasped the crowing receiver tighter against her lap.

"The upholsterers have arrived," Margherita announced, opening the door and sticking her head into the room. Lavinia started and hung up.

"What upholsterers?"

"No idea. But you should know. They are unloading a bunch of stuff from a van."

"May we come in?" a voice asked. The maid moved away from the door and two men walked into the room carrying a huge roll of white fabric.

"Good Lord!" Lavinia exclaimed. Margherita turned directly to the older upholsterer. "What's going to happen now?"

"We have come to do the job." He turned to Lavinia. "You said it was very urgent . . . have you changed your mind?"

"No, no." She remembered now. One day—which now seemed long ago—she had envisioned herself surrounded by a different living room—white linen, no pictures, no knick-knacks. She had even quit smoking, for a few weeks, since that was also part of the new program of life inspired by a crystal-clear, minimalist style. It had happened in the spring, when she had first guessed the real nature of the relationship between Sandro and the woman who owned a collection of contemporary art—the same one who had now conjured up the yacht and the tantalizing mouth that had lured him away from her. Lavinia suddenly remembered clearly when she had decided to redo the living room, and also why: twenty years of analysis had not helped her get better or make fewer mistakes, but they had made her constantly aware of what was going on at the deepest levels of her consciousness.

So, she had envisioned herself in a dazzling, aseptic frame; and upon this vision she had immediately based a plan—because there was nothing more comforting to her than setting up a plan. It meant that the future was not just a flaccid continuation of an awful present but something new and quite different.

She remembered how she had begged the upholsterer to

break all other commitments and rush to the rescue of her living room. Then she had completely forgotten about it.

From the balcony, Sigmund started scratching the door to be let in.

"I'm coming, dearest," Lavinia shouted in his direction. She placed an ashtray brimming with butts into Margherita's hand. "Here, take care of it. And, please, let the dog in . . . My God, my God . . . Coming!" she shrieked at the balcony.

Sigmund burst into the room, and immediately started gnawing the leg of a table.

"Time is money," the upholsterer said.

"I'm going to leave you the keys so you can take care of it while we are away," Lavinia proposed. Back from her vacation she would find the stage readied for a role whose cues she had already forgotten. Actually, only part of the stage would be different: the white upholstery. The rest would still be the usual mess: the marks of Sigmund's teeth everywhere, cigarette butts, bills, receipts in empty flower vases, empty ballpoint pens, a whole life full of mistakes, missed opportunities, guilt, a life that no amount of reupholstering would ever set straight. Besides, it was going to cost her a fortune, and, as was often the case, she would have to ask Violante to help her pay for something that no longer interested her.

Margherita was walking back into the living room with the clean ashtray. She stopped by the door, right behind the upholsterer, shaking her head and gesturing silent messages of disapproval to Lavinia. "I could stay until they have finished the job," she finally suggested. Sigmund had started barking at the roll of white fabric. By now the sun was at its highest; they would have to travel in the worst heat.

"That's impossible," Lavinia whined. "As I already told you, this year we are not staying at Villa Grande: I have asked Violante to get the Limonaia ready for us. Who is going to help me if you stay in Milan?"

Her nervous gastritis was knotting her stomach; the dog was

going crazy; the heat was getting worse by the minute; the upholsterer, his helper, and Margherita were looking at her reproachfully because she was the one who had created the mess and wasn't doing anything to clear it up.

"Sigmund, shut up!" she screamed. She handed one of the suitcases to the upholsterer. "Please, help us get out of here," she said. "Take your time, and when you are done, leave the keys with the doorman." As the two men left carrying the luggage, she tried to reassure Margherita. "Should anything belonging to you disappear, I'll take full responsibility for it," she whispered in her ear. "Don't worry, and let's go."

"My color TV . . ."

"Don't think about it. Get that beast and let's go."

It was a horrible trip. The heat was asphyxiating. Sigmund kept vomiting, Margherita kept obsessing about her beloved belongings abandoned to the dubious honesty of a stranger. "My calf-length beaver fur, my snakeskin handbag, my color TV . . ." The doleful list went on and on. Lavinia kept telling her that she was ready to take full responsibility for everything herself, but her words only elicited a smile full of bitterness, sarcasm, and spite. Margherita had been with Lavinia for twelve years, and, all things considered, was fond of her, but she still saw her as a middle-aged child and not as a reliable adult.

"My silver frame, my cashmere *princesse*, my Valentino suit. . . ."

Meanwhile, Sandro's plane—Lavinia had furiously checked the schedule—had landed in Athens and, at the terminal, Rosy-lips was triumphantly waving to him from beyond a glass partition.

The car sped out of the last tunnel. Lavinia saw the Alpi Apuane on her left and smelled the sea in the air.

"Yes," she said. "I'm going to fill the patio with shocking-pink flowers."

3

I DON'T NEED A STUDY in the city. The paintings I buy to resell I keep at home. Since my business, though large in value, is small in size, it requires a minimum amount of administration and I don't have to have a secretary.

All I need is a quiet room, a table, and a telephone on the ground floor of the Arnolfina—on the ground floor and toward the back, otherwise my curiosity regarding the Santini family would keep me away from my work, my eyes glued to the navy binoculars that I bought as an absolutely indispensable instrument the very day I moved into my new abode.

Today the temptation is stronger than ever. I would have noticed the excitement in the park even if I had not received Violante's note: I have to force myself to go down to my study.

The painting with the kingfisher stands in the middle of the room, in full light, leaning against a sturdy scaffolding. It was brought to me two years ago by a ragman who had found it in an unauthorized dump, one of the many fouling up our beautiful city. Painted on three panels, somewhat warped and roughly held together, it represented—when I first saw it—two blond women sitting at the foot of a tree, of which only the trunk was visible, its foliage vanishing beyond the upper edge of the painting. The ground was stony and bare but for a tuft of bullrushes growing out of the lower right corner. Perched on one of these, its wings barely raised as if about to take flight, was the kingfisher.

The painting—in terrible condition—was simple but full of grace. As I had paid very little for it, I was immediately pleased with the deal; little did I know that, once the painting was cleaned, the entire scene would take on a new meaning that would mark the beginning of one of the most exciting professional ventures in my life.

On what I had at first mistaken for a tree trunk appeared, right at the upper edge of the painting, two nailed feet; and the two women—whose clothes and general shabbiness I had also misinterpreted—were not sitting but kneeling. In other words, I was no longer looking at an Arcadian scene but a religious painting, the lower part of a crucifixion. Given the quality of the style—neat but quite primitive—I was sure that the painting must have come from a poor country church, but which one? It did not look Tuscan, not even Italian; but I couldn't believe that such a modest, and at the same time bulky, work could have been carried across the Alps, or even moved from one region to the next: it made no sense.

And it had the oddest proportions. Even though mutilated, it was incredibly long and narrow, and it was obviously missing at least three or four more panels representing the body of Christ, and maybe a strip of sky above the cross. Such dimensions couldn't have befitted any of the old churches in the region, except perhaps one—now somewhat dilapidated but still bearing the traces of some ancient, rustic beauty—in a small village of the high Val Freddana that had grown out of a lansquenet camp around the sixteenth century

It was by sheer chance that I thought of that church, but the moment I did everything fell into place, including the northern characteristics of the painting. I combed through the entire area:

not just the ruins of the old church but houses, stables, neighboring villages. I found fragments of ancient murals, painted boards, and an entire wardrobe decorated with hunting scenes. Like a trademark, the blue-green bird appeared in all my finds. Everything pointed to the existence of a local sixteenth-century painter, of obvious Germanic origin, who signed his works with a small kingfisher in the lower right corner.

I have spent two years on the subject and now all I've left to do is to write a definitive draft and publish it.

Silvana has just brought me a cup of coffee, as she always does when she sees I have started working. All the Mauritians of the area are related: Sonny, Fatima, and Chris, their father at Villa Grande. Through them, news travels quickly from one house to the next. But Silvana is the one who gathers all the rumors up, and every morning delivers them to me while pouring my second cup of coffee of the day.

"This summer Signora Lavinia will be staying at the Limonaia," she tells me.

"How come, after such a long time?!"

Silvana sighs. "And yet it feels like yesterday."

For me, instead, it is as if centuries had gone by. What now? Now everything should start anew, but in a different way, I hope.

So, Lavinia is again going to take over what, twenty-three years ago, had been her home for just a few days, the length of her tragic marriage with Filippo, Violante's eldest son. I hadn't yet bought the Arnolfina. I was renting a handsome flat in the city, and Violante was only a client who hadn't yet accepted me among her friends. But I knew her sons well, even though Filippo was a little older and Leopoldo much younger than I. Already then, Lavinia responded to my adoration by confiding in me about her heartaches, of which her own marriage was most prodigal.

I saw her often, ran to her side at the merest snap of her fingers, and sent her huge baskets of flowers, while she—in just a few months—went through that entire terrible event, from the short engagement to the absurd wedding, Filippo's desertion, his tragic death, Nicola's birth.

She lived at Villa Grande, where she had sought Violante's protection just a few days after their return from the honeymoon. The Limonaia was closed, and closed it stayed.

Violante took care of the child. Lavinia enrolled in the university, dropped out when she was only halfway through, tried other things to fill her days. She moved to Milan right at the time when I bought the Arnolfina. Nicola remained with his grandmother, which was a reason for Lavinia to come to Tuscany quite often, though always as Violante's guest.

I take the reopening of the Limonaia as a favorable sign. Nothing, not even cannon shots, could keep me away from my tower right now. I immediately return to my room and try to interpret this last portent while, with my binoculars, I watch the two hired farmhands take care of the cleaning.

It is Nives, in her blue uniform, who orders them about. Her voice reaches me loud and clear. Nives has been my last article of faith. Indeed, she is the real right thing. Unfortunately, she can't be acquired, nor copied. No counterfeiter could imitate her satisfactorily, as I soon learned. Naturally, it was a bitter discovery, but as I was making it, I felt a certain gratification. I told myself that having the subtlety necessary to understand it was already something.

It happened on the occasion of Violante's seventieth birthday party. My book on the Master of the *Virgin in Red* had just come out. In other words, I was not exactly a nonentity; nevertheless I overflowed—literally—with gratitude for that invitation. I was even afraid that it would show, maybe in the form of some embarrassing liquefaction which the lady of the house would surely fail to appreciate. Just one week earlier, following an auction sale of Chinese porcelain, I had briefly stopped to chat with her and a few other people. Among them was a loquacious and somewhat fanatic woman who had been raving about a new book. "It drips with blood and tears," she had said. At which, Violante, barely raising an eyebrow, had replied, "I disapprove of anyone oozing organic fluids in public."

Is gratitude an organic fluid? I wondered as, not without some apprehension, I climbed the steps of villa Santini on the evening of Violante's birthday party.

As usual, a servant stood by the door to welcome the guests. I had recently summoned one of his brothers from Mauritius to come and fulfill similar functions at the Arnolfina. It was a special evening, a real reception, with women in full-length gowns and so on and so forth; but the most discreet and yet unmistakable sign of the exceptionality of the gathering was the presence, next to the servant—or rather, three steps behind him, toward the drawing room, in an intermediary position between him and the lady of the house—of a new character, who had just stepped out of the darkness, but who obviously had long been part of the house. Dressed in a long black gown, elegant but simple with the appropriate neckline, she accompanied the women to the cloakroom, where she undoubtedly provided them with all they needed: brushes, needles and thread, news, bits of advice. She also marked the clear-cut and insurmountable division between Violante's more recent acquaintances and her ancient, inherited friends: the latter addressed the black-clad figure by name—Nives—and hugged her, while, bestowing a very special smile on them, she inquired about their children and distant grandchildren.

Her presence in that house seemed an established fact. In a flash, two parallel genealogical trees appeared in front of my searching eyes, the witnesses of a slow progress, as slow as the establishment of any true nobility. Maybe Nives's mother, if not her grandmother, a rustic creature with smooth apple cheeks, had been the first to come down from her native mountains to work as a maid in the house. By and by, in the course of each individual life and through generations, the role had grown in prestige—from maid, to housekeeper, to governess—

until it had become something special, a beloved, irreplaceable figure, connected to the house by bonds stronger than blood. A painting can be bought, as can a precious stone—not to mention a vicuna overcoat, I thought as I entrusted mine to the boy whose tanned face so resembled that of my Sonny. How could I have believed it really meant something? It could be bought with money, but Nives could only be inherited.

All this I merely intuited that evening, in a flash of clairvoyance; but I had time to put order to my thoughts during the following days, when Violante was ill—nothing serious, just a long, ugly flu. Like a good neighbor, every morning on my way to the city I stopped at the villa to inquire about her health, and asked to speak with Nives. She received me in a small parlor next to the vestibule: an ironing board, a desk with a telephone, a file cabinet, two armchairs, a television set. From this room, she governed the house and oversaw the execution of Violante's supreme instructions.

She would offer me a cup of coffee and speak to me of the lady, with great concern at first, while I affectionately reassured her: "But my dear, she is such a strong woman she will bury us all." Then she gradually grew more hopeful and serene, until at last one morning she met me with a smile. "I think you may pay her a short visit."

She accompanied me into Violante's room. The old lady was in bed, leaning against three pillows. She offered me a hand that looked as withered and crinkled as a bird's foot.

"I'm really fed up with being sick. Tomorrow I'm getting up."

"No way," Nives retorted.

And the two women started bickering—though that is not the right word, evoking, as it does, petulant sounds, whereas theirs was like a cooing of doves, which I eagerly took in, stunned by the joy of being allowed to witness an expression of such a long intimacy.

After which I did not find peace until I provided myself with a convincing simulacrum of Nives in the guise of a married couple in their fifties, on whom I had had my eye for quite a while before finally hiring them.

In the past, Piero and Silvana had respectively been the gardener and the cook's helper in Violante Santini's house; then they had married and taken over the tobacco shop in their village. For the next twenty-five years, they had lived in two small rooms right above the shop. My proposal reached them at the right time, when their son, having just gotten engaged, was waiting to find a job and a home before getting married. So, Piero and Silvana left him their apartment and their business and accepted the lucrative job I had offered them along with totally independent living quarters above the garage.

From that day on, until I was sure I had done everything in my power, I relentlessly worked on them with the same expertise—I would even say genius—with which, at the beginning of my career, I had upgraded so many common kitchen cupboards into "credenze Veneziane": in six months, Piero and Silvana came as close to being a couple of old and faithful servants as they possibly could. All the holes were filled with money, all undesirable protuberances were rounded off and smoothed down with daily applications of kindness and respect—ingredients I can use liberally since I am rich and my soul is naturally kind and respectful.

I don't think Piero and Silvana ever quite understood the real meaning of my enterprise. But they immediately figured out the precise extent of its aspirations, and, having made sure that the idyllic landscape that had been proposed to them as the locale of our relationship was exactly what it seemed and hid no traps, they helped me speed through the various stages of solidarity and affection, and in less than a year granted me what only a few servants grant to only a few masters during a lifetime spent under the same roof. In return, they received what is generally proffered in such instances, from the generous check for the newborn grandchild, to an affectionate tolerance for their whims—"So long, old boy," I would hastily say, shaking influential hands. "This evening I can't be late for dinner. My Silvana would never forgive me if I made her miss a single word of *Dynasty*."

4

VIOLANTE DECIDED TO SEE for herself. She glanced at the watch. She had all the time in the world. On the phone, Lavinia had said that she would be leaving early to travel during the cooler part of the day, but that was the sort of thing she always said and—for some reason or other—never did.

She took the shears, the basket, the gloves. She went through the vegetable garden where there was an area devoted to flowers for the house. While she was gathering them, she resolved to send a basketful to Lavinia every morning to avoid the havoc her daughter-in-law generally wreaked on the flower beds of the garden: brutally tearing off the stems, treading on just about everything, and usually abandoning her droopy, warm booty at the foot of a statue, on a bench, or on the roof of a car, where it would just lie, dying. She was unable to measure the duration of her passions: she would enthusiastically start something new, only to quit midway, discouraged by the most obvious and predictable difficulties.

On the other hand, Lavinia was unable to measure anything. Everything she owned was inevitably either too large or too small, she always did things either too early or too late, to say nothing of the way she spent money. When Nicola was born, everybody thought it was a blessing, albeit in the middle of a great misfortune, that Lavinia—barely twenty years old and eager to start anew after her terrible experience with Filippo— couldn't wish for anything better than to entrust her child to his grandmother.

Nicola: Violante felt the same pang she had felt when she had first held him in her arms. He had been such a quiet baby, never causing any trouble, as if he had wanted to apologize for being in the world. Then, he had become a good child, and now, at twenty-two, he was already a sensible young man, studious, kind, patient.

Her shears snipped the long stem of a brick-red zinnia. Still, one had to know when to quit. Everything had to be put back in its rightful place: feelings, blood ties, priorities. By the end of the summer, everything had to be in order, so that she would have a chance to see it with her own eyes.

It was strange that she so often dreamed of Nicola and La-vinia as if they were brother and sister, and both her children. Indeed, as she got older, something still odder happened to her even when she was awake: she saw the characters of the family portrait, of which she herself was part, take each other's place, overlap, split in two. In her memory, the two men who slept side by side in the country cemetery—her husband and Filippo, her older son—fused into one person, a beloved spouse who had died tragically, leaving her a whole array of children, in-cluding, besides the two sons to whom she had actually given birth, Lavinia and Nicola.

In that family portrait, only Leopoldo and Cynthia were at their rightful places. Leopoldo, her second and last son: Vi-olante loved him with a will, as if to make up for never having loved him quite as much as his brother. And then there was Cynthia, the other daughter-in-law, the providential American who, with her dollars, had rescued the paper mill and restored the family finances.

Leopoldo had been so madly in love with her when he first introduced her to Violante. It was in the summer; Cynthia, with her white gloves and not one hair out of place, looked so irrepressibly and intimately clean—so much cleaner than anything else around her—that Violante had wondered whether she had received all the appropriate vaccinations and would be able to survive in a Latin atmosphere. She too had looked very much in love, despite her Anglo-Saxon reserve.

Something had gone wrong even in that marriage: politely, without tragedies. Nobody had confided in her—nor, surely, in anybody else—but she knew that even they were not doing well. "Doing well": Violante was much too reasonable to make plans of happiness either for herself or for others, but she felt it was her right to wish that her loved ones were at least "doing well."

She didn't have much time left. Everything cohered in her plan, but whereas she knew some of its elements well—all those relating to Lavinia and Nicola—she still had no clear terms for those concerning Leopoldo and Cynthia. What on earth was wrong with those two?

The French windows of the Limonaia were wide open. A great deal of furniture had been stacked upside down on the patio. Helped by two farmhands, Nives brushed, dusted, polished. Seeing Violante approach, she stopped and smiled at her.

"We are almost done," she said. "All we have left to do is to put this stuff back in, and that's it."

She went into the house to get two crystal vases; she filled them with water at the garden faucet and placed them on the stone table in the center of the patio. "While you prepare the vases, we are going to carry the furniture back where it belongs."

The vases were absolutely right for the flowers she had picked. Violante started dipping the stems into the water one by one. Nives kept ordering the men about, striding up and down the patio with a sure step. Her voice rang with a lively Emilian accent.

You will never abandon them, my old friend, Violante thought. Then, out loud, she said, "They have never lived here in the summer. I wonder whether it will be too hot for them."

Nives interrupted her work for a while and stood by Violante, staring at the open windows with her. The two women sighed. The newlyweds had only spent a few days in the Limonaia, after which Lavinia—crushed and forlorn—had sought shelter in the villa. Shortly thereafter, Filippo had forever untied the knot of that impossible marriage by driving off a highway viaduct.

Everything had been so brutally convenient, it was outright horrible.

"It's very sunny," Nives noted. "But when the awnings are up, it should be all right." Together, they walked into the living room just as the men were placing the sofa back onto the freshly polished brick floor. "I have done everything as you told me to, aside from Nicky's stuff. After all, we have time to think it over until Saturday."

"I have told you I have made up my mind. Nicola will live here with his mother."

She could not reveal her plans to Nives, and show her the diagram. She would have looked at it with her usual skepticism. There were times when Nives's good sense was depressing, and this was not the moment for her to lose confidence. Everything had to be organized according to her deepest convictions, as if it were a precise ritual with its own ineluctable laws whose logic and validity no one would ever dream of questioning. In this particular instance, the ceremony was the abdication of an old queen.

"You can at least start by having some of his stuff moved in—his stereo, for instance. Whatever you want. Then we'll think about the rest."

5

THE FURNITURE was authentic, but smothered under such a profusion of lace, velvet, and satin that the room looked like the dressing room of a chanteuse. Fatima—thin, dark, and dressed all in white—walked in with the breakfast tray. She placed it on Cynthia's knees and stood by her bedside.

"Madame Lavinia arrive aujourd'hui," she said.

Cynthia yawned. "I know. I was at my mother-in-law's yesterday, when she called."

"On m'a dit qu'elle habitera la Limonaia."

"Out of the question."

"Mais oui, madame. Nives et les hommes sont déjà là pour préparer la maison. Madame Violante a apporté les fleurs."

"I don't believe it. Is monsieur still in?"

"Oui, madame."

"Then go fetch him for me, quick. No, wait. I'll go myself. Hand me my robe."

She swooped down on him in a cloud of pink chiffon. He was already at the door, about to go out.

"Hold it," she said, threateningly.

"What is it?"

"Not here. Let's go into the library."

Leopoldo sighed. "All right. But I have only a few minutes."

They walked into the library, but he held her back by the door, refusing to sit down. "I'm listening."

"Lavinia has reopened the Limonaia."

"So?"

"Did you know?"

"No, I didn't."

"Fatima just told me."

Leopoldo remained silent, waiting for her to go on.

"Did you hear what I said?" Cynthia asked after a while.

"What?"

Cynthia sighed. "Of course not. You haven't understood a thing. She is arriving in one hour and I have just heard about it from Fatima. From my maid, who heard it from Nives. In other words, I find out what goes on in this family through the servants. Now do you understand what I am talking about?"

Leopoldo did not understand. His wife's grievances had almost always seemed to him both perfectly justified and totally absurd. They were like her hair dryers, her blenders, her toasters, and all the other supermodern gadgets she had brought back from America: wonderful but inoperable on the Italian electric outlets, at least without the intermediary of a transformer.

"I knew nothing about it either. Why should you care to know what Lavinia is doing in advance?"

"I don't believe you," Cynthia sighed.

"I've got someone strong and fair/ who is waiting for me there/down in Santa Fe," she mentally recited. Oh, if she could only ditch that bunch of snobbish parasites, if she could only humiliate them by showing them how much happier she could be elsewhere—among clear, open faces, loyal hearts, simpler rules, and impeccable sanitary facilities, in other words, in Columbus, Ohio. But what would happen to her, far from all these people, things, trees, streets? Leopoldo's aquiline profile, dark hair, and long thin hands; Lavinia's drawl; the flutter of the wind in the olive trees; Violante sitting at the head of the table during one of her dinners; Nives scolding Nicola for bringing home another stray dog; the old paper mill that had belonged to the family for three centuries and was still plugging away next to all the other new plants; the wardrobes full of linen sheets and towels; the Ferragosto procession winding its way through the garden . . . She would miss it all. She could leave, but she would come back, if only for the sake of discipline. Here was a world that was about to end and they, its legitimate children, didn't even notice. Maybe, by now, it was only a wax museum, but even if that were the case somebody had to see to its upkeep—with good will and respect.

"Come on, come on. No point getting into a tizzy over such nonsense," Leopoldo said. Then he added, "I won't be back for lunch. I'll see you this evening. Don't forget we are having dinner at Villa Grande."

"You don't keep me informed about what's going on in the family because you don't see me. It's as if I were invisible. I am no longer in Columbus, Ohio, but I am not here either. I am nowhere."

She pushed the door wide open and yelled, "Fatima! I'll be waiting for you upstairs."

She strode past Leopoldo and rushed upstairs, a hand clasped to her heart, her pale skin flushed by anger, her porcelain eyes shining with tears. She let herself drop onto her bed, face up, her fists denting the pillow on each side of her head, and did not move: she looked like a newborn princess in a frilly baby-gown on the day of her first public appearance.

She kept her eyes fixed on the velvet-ribboned tulle canopy, focusing them on the very point where the folds, converging, formed a sort of vortex. I am all alone, and maybe he no longer loves me. Could it be he no longer loves me? These were the rearguard of melancholy thoughts that gradually scattered and vanished into the darkness at the end of the huge, empty hall she was cleaning up. Following her doctor's instructions, without turning her eyes away she started concentrating all her attention, memory, and intelligence on just one point, letting her mind pucker into a sort of navel, like the one formed by the tulle of the canopy above her. At this point, she was ready to begin one of the mnemonic exercises of self-hypnosis, it made no difference which one. She liked to make up lists of names.

"Asher, Benjamin, Dan, Gad, Issachar, Joseph, Judah, Levi, Naphtali, Reuben, Simeon, Zebulun." She articulated every name syllable by syllable, breathing deeply after each one. Her fists began to relax. "How I love him," she said. Now she could think about it without suffering. She did love him, even though her love had little to do with that glorified emotion that was supposed to be at once compact and yet miraculously multiform, and to consist of elements whose proximity seemed to her both impossible and profane—crude lust and pure tenderness (of the kind she felt for Leopoldo), the most revolting physical prurience and the most angelic spiritual impulses, all at the same moment, all inspired by the same person as one total feeling. Was it possible? Either the entire world was privy to a colossal lie or it was the truth, in which case she lacked whatever it was—a gland, a humor—that could metabolize everything into a homogeneous compound.

Fatima entered the room and, with controlled, harmonious movements, started preparing the apparatus for the physiotherapeutical morning ritual, during which, without scenes or complications, both Cynthia's elementary libido and the sophisticated requirements related to her personal care were simultaneously satisfied. Among aromatic oils, white linen towels, rubber tubes, and shining bowls, a light flutter, like the flapping of diaphanous wings, would eventually occur somewhere within Cynthia's bowels, assuring at once the rosy smoothness of her Anglo-Saxon complexion, the regularity of her intestines, her muscle tone, and the proper irrigation of her scalp.

Cynthia never even wondered whether Fatima was aware of the side effects of her treatments; the expressions of her pleasure were so subtle that she herself almost forgot them the moment they were over and she could abandon herself to the neutral contentment of a well-tended baby.

6

HE CARRIED a rolled sleeping bag slightly askew across his shoulders—a simple affair, without the metallic frame used by today's hitchhikers. He held it in place with one hand while, with the other, he waved a red-willow stick on the tip of which he had left a tuft of silvery leaves. He wore tight jeans whose hue, like that of the shirt, was worn down to an indefinable sheerness which the eye of the observer could color as it pleased. His were the exact opposite of the emperor's clothes: real, but easily transformed or eliminated by the imagination. I am saying this because seen from a distance, the slender limbs of the boy suggested total nudity, whereas his entire figure—his raised arm, the oblong object resting on his shoulders, the stick, and the general impression of lightness and luminosity—reminded me of one of my earlier forgeries, a Mannerist *Good Shepherd* that I arbitrarily reinvented some thirty years ago by deftly connecting the few crusts of color left on an old canvas. That work had marked the beginning of a new era, since that's when I first got the idea of executing, in addition to the fake an art dealer had commissioned, a duly aged fake of the fake itself. I sold the latter on my own to a rich German merchant who had come to Montecatini for the baths, and, much to my surprise, it brought me twice as much as the art dealer had paid me for the other canvas. After that experience, I set up my own business, and even made a few memorable deals—of which, of course, I can't yet speak freely, not even after thirty years. But the luckiest of them all—even though I did not realize it until later—was that the more I forged great art, the better I got to know it, so that I have now become a world-renowned expert on the subject, and definitely the highest authority in all that concerns Italian painting.

I spotted the boy who looks like the Good Shepherd a few minutes ago from my tower: I was getting dressed to go downtown while keeping an eye on the intense activity around the Limonaia. He was coming up the road that skirts the walls of Violante's park.

He walked slowly; I went downstairs, started the car, drove down my driveway and out the gate in the time it took him to reach the top of the climb and find himself right in front of me.

With his hand he signals me to stop.

"Excuse me . . ."

"Yes?"

"I'm looking for Nicola Santini."

"He is not here, he is in America. He should be back in a week."

He does not seem too disappointed. He shrugs his knapsack back in place. "In any case, this is where he lives, right? I mean, his family has a house around here."

I have already recognized him as a member of that immense freemasonry of young people who travel around the world visiting each other and do not hesitate, when they need a place to sleep, to call on their friends' parents, or friends of friends, dropping in on people they have never met before, without references to speak of but always ready to be turned down and go knock on the next door.

"Yes," I tell him. "His house is right inside this park. If you follow this wall, you'll find the gate right around the next bend. There are three houses: Nicola's grandmother lives in the largest one, his uncle in the second largest, and his mother in the smallest."

The boy smiles, lowering his head and looking askance at me; the shadow around his eyes is light blue, almost silver.

"Like the three bears," he says. This is exactly what I thought last night while gazing at the Santini park from the top of my tower; but coming from him, the observation sounds so unbearably quaint that I pretend I haven't heard it. This boy inspires me with the sort of diffidence I immediately feel toward anyone who is trying to please me. I see him as one of those professional seducers who are unable to utter the simplest sentence without assuming a persuasive tone of voice and repeatedly batting their eyelashes. I can't believe he is a friend of Nicola's. Nicola is tall, strong, diligent, loyal. He is naturally kind to everybody, but doesn't worry about the impression he makes on others.

I leave the globetrotter on the dusty edge of the road and head on toward Lucca. I try to remember how I was at his and Nicola's age: I was very different.

In those days, I was swimming against the tide, with all my might and the will my mother had bestowed on me as if it had been a material asset, a family treasure to bequeath to one's offspring. I knew what I wanted to leave behind—the ungracefully oblique kitchen with its opaque sounds and the smell of poverty—just as I knew, with increasing clarity, that my goal was not a pharmacy counter; but it took me several more years before I actually knew what it was. A school diploma, a "proper" job, and a reasonably comfortable life as one's highest aspirations seemed to me even sadder than a chipped cup with a greenish rim.

Oddly enough, what was supposed to be a very humble means to a precise end—a sort of piggy bank to break open, empty out, and throw away—instead turned out to be the road to the realization of my mother's and my dreams. It was the inheritance left me by my father—a little man with the soul of a loser—that finally led me to fame and fortune.

That little man, of whom I have so few memories, had a small laboratory with the most elementary equipment, where he fixed pottery. My mother had always helped him, and therefore was fairly well acquainted with the trade. At the end of the war, she resumed working even more intensely than before since the antiquarian market, then in full upswing, permitted it and my studies in pharmacy demanded it. I studied a great deal, but had enough time to help her, and pretty soon started to lend a very personal touch to our activity.

It turned out I had an artistic hand. I quickly moved from pottery to enameled furniture, from that to the restoration of paintings, and from restoration to forgery. I crossed this last threshold the day a Roman art dealer asked me to clean up the portrait of a woman by Artemisia Gentileschi. It was a beautiful piece, but impossible to sell because the woman in the painting held a skull in her hand. As a result, people loved to look at it but did not dare buy it, no doubt put off by that macabre touch.

"A mere brushstroke," the art dealer kept saying, "would do the trick."

So, without bringing any alteration to the rosy arm and the position of the hand, I turned the skull into a mirror: it took only a couple of brushstrokes, the faintest tampering, and the art dealer sold the painting for the price he wanted.

At first, I had some qualms, somewhat shared by the art dealer, while my mother, who as a rule was a moralist, had none. According to her, the aim of a painting was to provide pleasure to the eyes: any painting fulfilling this requirement was, in her mind, honest and authentic.

"They are not blind. If they buy it, it means they like it, don't you think? Stop worrying and follow your nose."

Then there was the stratagem of the *Good Shepherd*, after which I started working on my own. At twenty-three, though I had only a few exams to go, I quit pharmacy. The university degree that's hanging on the wall behind my desk was not earned the usual way: it is *honoris causa* and was awarded to me last January, by the department of art history at the University of Perugia in appreciation of my work on the Master of the *Virgin in Red.*

Since I quit the profession of forger at the age of thirty, I have been simultaneously an art dealer and a scholar. I like to think that this change of activity has helped create two images of me that reciprocally enhance each other: the more garish and rascally aspects of the forger are somewhat upgraded and ennobled by the sound scholarship of the dealer, while the professorial grayness of the latter is lent gloss and color by the former.

I am sure, as I get out of my Volvo and place its keys in the hands of the garage attendant, that I have come a very long way since the crooked kitchen of my early youth, and that I can now definitely say I have arrived: indeed, today, I am very much like one of the people seated at the table I observed through the crack in the shutter, in the summer of 1944.

7

THEY ARRIVED at four, exhausted by the heat.

"Mrs. Santini is resting," Nives told them. "She left word to call her. Anyway, she generally wakes up around this time," she added, glancing at her watch. "Then, when you are ready, you can go to the Limonaia. We have straightened it up and the key is in the door." She took Margherita to her parlor and let Lavinia go to Violante's bedroom by herself. Filippo's widow was at home there, and did not need to be announced: this was what the governess had wisely left unsaid, Lavinia thought as she crossed the living room. And yet she did not feel at all as if those rooms belonged to her; rather, she felt that she belonged to them, worthless as she was and so totally unfit for anything. Twenty years earlier she had been unable to deserve Filippo's love, and now, here she was, late as usual, perspiring, unhappy, her belly all twisted up and swollen, dragging herself under the suspicious eyes of the portraits decorating the walls.

"Darling!"

"Did I wake you up?"

"No. I was reading. I am so happy to see you. Come sit next to me." Violante had always felt a great tenderness for that tall, clumsy child; and then Filippo—her firstborn, and only true love—had started treating her so obnoxiously that even the most natural movements of her heart were overcome by pity. Confronted with such abominable behavior, she had been unable to take her son's side, but she couldn't have remained neutral either: she had felt compelled to make a choice, and she had chosen Lavinia. She had taken her under her roof and had treated her like a sick kitten. She had also ordered all the doors of the Limonaia bolted for fear Filippo might come and carry out his evil practices right under that poor child's nose. Filippo had not come back; indeed, she had never seen him again, not even the little that was left of him after the accident. And she had never been able to get rid of the thought that he might have sped off that viaduct precisely because she had taken her support away from him, even if with reason. With reason? Can one speak of reason in such matters? And yet, at the time she had felt she had done the right thing; and since her choice had been so hard, she had even considered it noble, a behavior full of ancient virtue, worthy of a Roman matriarch. It had taken her years to realize that it was all wrong, that there are natural bonds that go beyond mere reason.

But that's what had happened, and she could not go back. The only thing that she could do now was to go all the way: if she had traded Filippo for Lavinia, then she might as well love her as a daughter.

Violante looked at Lavinia, trying to find something in her appearance she could say something flattering, encouraging about; but she found nothing. Her blond hair was hanging limply on each side of her long, white face. Lavinia, whose color could be either silvery or ashen, depending on the angle of the light, and whose long limbs could appear either sensuously fluid or awkwardly angular, occupied, on the scale of feminine beauty—and according to Violante's secret opinion—a variable place somewhere between Botticelli's *Primavera* and the bony spinsters of some English novels, first and foremost David Copperfield's great-aunt Betsey Trotwood. A trifle was enough to make her shift in either direction, and today she was definitely closer to Betsy.

Violante gave up the idea of complimenting her. "Filippo's friend died," she said instead. "We knew she was old, but try to guess how old she actually was."

"Dead?" It was such a long time since Lavinia had given a single thought to the woman who had so atrociously humiliated her that, to her, she could have been dead for years. When Filippo had driven off that viaduct, it was as though he had left this world clasped in a deathly embrace with his permanent mistress, the very one Lavinia had been unable to supplant if only for one day, though she was only twenty—and she had counted on this as an unconquerable weapon of seduction—and Filippo already thirty-five.

Literally, not even for one day, since immediately after the marriage ceremony they had left on their honeymoon and, with no explanation, he had decided to stop after only nine miles, in Pisa, where they had arrived around two in the afternoon. That is where Filippo had fulfilled his marital duty, as if it were some minor office surgery. Neither of them had fully undressed, and the whole thing had happened so quickly that their bodies had barely rumpled the burgundy-and-white-striped bedspread they had not had the time to remove.

The previous summer, Lavinia had often gone dancing in Versilia, where Peppino di Capri sang and played the piano while standing—like someone who is only passing through and, having other pressing obligations, doesn't even bother to take a seat. Somehow she thought of him while her new husband, whom she really found somewhat ripe and out of breath—the very reasons that had made her hope he would love her tenderly and forever—was settling his debt with her, and decided that if anyone ever asked her how she had made love the first time, she would say, "Like Peppino di Capri."

Having done his duty, Filippo had left her alone in the hotel and had not reappeared until the following morning. Then, after a few depressing days on Elba—which he had spent mostly on the phone—he had confessed, or rather, had voluptuously thrown in her face that he had spent their wedding night with Mafalda, who had deflowered him when he was eighteen, and had always been and would always be his mistress and his love, something everybody knew except, ironically enough, her, Lavinia. "How could you have ever imagined"— he had stared at her with the cruelest eyes—"how could you have fooled yourself into believing that I would ever love you?" And then had added other terrible things that she had tried desperately to forget and hadn't even been able to repeat to Violante.

"She was only three years younger than I. Can you believe it? Of course, I was a very young mother for Filippo—just imagine, I lost two of my milk teeth while I was expecting him. Still, it is unbelievable that he could have so totally lost his head over a woman who was almost his mother's age. But maybe not, maybe it isn't at all unbelievable. Les amours des autres, who's to say!" Then, with a coy smile, she added, "Besides, let's not forget that Filippo was an inveterate mamma's boy. Anyway, what about your own love life? How are things with your sociologist?"

"Ghastly," Lavinia sniffed disconsolately. "He's off on a cruise with someone else. I caught a glimpse of her last winter. Nothing special, believe me. At times I feel so disgusted that I'd do anything to get out of it . . . at least, emotionally. You see, I'd like to be able to see him as a man I like and with whom I don't mind spending an evening now and then."

"That's exactly what you should do."

Lavinia leaned back in her armchair and turned her eyes to the chandelier.

"I know, I know. On the other hand, you see, these other women come and go, whereas he has been with me for over three years. And there are times when it is all so perfect, and he seems so . . . how shall I put it . . . so close and devoted. . . . Oh, I don't know."

Violante snorted. "The problem with you, Lavinia, is that you are like those poor little maidens, so common in other times, who seemed destined to be robbed of all their savings by their suitors. There were thousands of them, and those rascals could smell them a mile away. One could not let them out of one's sight, not for a second, they couldn't be allowed out by themselves, they had to be treated like children, and even that did not help. They always ended up the same way. They used to worry us sick, Nives and me. You should ask her sometime, she knows something about it."

Lavinia crossed her arms over her belly trying to still the cramps. "If that's the way I am, and you may be right," she replied petulantly, "then I might as well stay with Sandro. Otherwise I will be treated exactly the same way by someone else, someone I might not even like as much." She tilted her head sideways; her intelligent gray eyes started smiling, then, suddenly, her whole face lit up. "In any case, I am delighted to be here, and quite curious to see if I can survive on my own at the Limonaia."

"I think that was a very wise decision."

They could hear Sigmund barking at the butterflies on the lawn. Cicadas filled the air with their consumptive chant.

"I'm going to leave Margherita here with Nives," Lavinia said. "She'll join me later. But now I am sneaking out of here to take possession of my home by myself."

8

THE HOUSE, WHERE THE LEMON TREES in their terra-cotta pots had once wintered, was on a level with the large stone patio. When Lavinia and Filippo were about to get married, Violante had let them choose which of the other two buildings in the park—Villa Piccola or the Limonaia—they wanted to inhabit. In fact, they could have also chosen the Arnolfina— which had not yet been sold to Aldo and had no name—an abandoned farm which, owing to its odd cylindrical tower, occupied a very privileged position right beyond the park walls.

Lavinia had been the one to choose the Limonaia over Villa Piccola, which should have naturally come to her as the first-born's wife, as well as over the Arnolfina, which, being situated outside the park, was the most independent of the three and, as a result, the best suited for bringing up one's own family, touched by, but not directly exposed to, Violante's maternal radiance.

She had chosen the Limonaia—or so she thought then— precisely because she liked the way its arched windows opened directly onto the patio. "I love the fact that there is hardly any distinction between the inside and the outside," she had said.

"An environmental continuum," as architectural journals called it, and that year architects reigned supreme. Indeed, they were the ones who decided whether or not someone had the right to be happy, depending on the structure and the furnishings of one's habitation. Since the newly built villas looked like lemon houses, Lavinia thought that to live in a real one would give her a better chance at happiness.

"It will rain inside the house, and the water will seep in through the doors," Filippo had predicted. That was probably the only time they had behaved like most other couples: they had quarreled for a while about a practical issue concerning their future together.

When Filippo gave in, she congratulated herself for her victory. Obviously he loved her so much, he was so enthralled with his young fiancée that he was ready to satisfy her every wish. This is what she told herself. Indeed, she even liked to think that her choice had been totally illogical—a whim, a quirk—as it made his capitulation still more flattering to her.

It didn't take her long to realize that Filippo's acquiescence meant something quite different from what she had hoped. He wanted an official wife, a legitimate heir, a socially acceptable façade, no question about it, but not a conventional marriage, not a daily intimacy involving the sharing of common territory. Since he had no intention of giving up his essentially celibate program of life, it was hardly worth his while to get involved in long discussions concerning the appropriateness of the conjugal domicile.

The arched windows appeared right around the bend. Unless, Lavinia thought, she had chosen it unconsciously, not so much to satisfy an aesthetic fancy but because she felt that to live in that sort of summer tea house was a way of remaining connected to the main house. The Limonaia was so obviously an annex of Villa Grande—fragile, almost temporary, the sort of place that could be abandoned at a moment's notice in favor of a real house. In fact, more than Filippo, she had wanted to marry the family—this was one of the many useless things she had found out in the course of her analysis—first of all Violante; then the old, paternal *Ingegner* Santini, who seemed to be one with his paper mill; then Leopoldo, her coeval, still a university student who liked to flirt with her, innocently, like a big affectionate puppy; and finally Nives, the servants, the farmhands—that entire, closed world that had so miraculously opened up to let her in and welcome her home, at last, she who since birth had felt doomed to be forever and everywhere a stranger.

She tore off a flower and started crumpling it in her hands. Everywhere, except in that garden, people seemed to be able to reach levels of intimacy among themselves which she could never even hope to attain with anyone. Allusions to past events, references to absent characters always baffled her: they were generally events and people she knew—as she, unheeded, inevitably hastened to assert—but always somewhat obliquely, never as closely as others seemed to. Where on earth was she at the magic instant of those fateful occurrences that had had the power to cement friendships, found undying memories, and, ultimately, confer on one that right of appurtenance that she would never possess?

Lavinia sat down on a stone bench whose back sunk into a thick, perfumed bush of angelica. What was the reason she always arrived everywhere late, when the chips were down and the polls were closed? Everywhere except in the blessed embrace of that garden. That was why it was so comforting, now and then, to go back to Violante's kingdom. What she had realized a little earlier as she was crossing the rooms of the villa was absolutely true: it was not the kingdom that belonged to her but she who belonged to the kingdom . . . yet it was such a comfort, if not to possess, to belong. To belong as intimately as she belonged to that family. With a shiver of deep satisfaction, she became aware of her undisputed superiority over Cynthia—the prom queen from Columbus, Ohio, former head cheerleader, all sequins and paper pom-poms, the darling of country clubs, and, even today, after ten years of exile, the proud recipient of tons of air mail—who, in the Santini microcosm, was still somewhat of an incongruity, a precious but poorly set stone, with a different refraction index and the wrong sparkle.

Lavinia left her perfumed niche and resumed her walk toward the Limonaia. It was a one-story building, but rather large, as it comprised, beside the lemon house, the former horse stable as well. Renovated, it had easily accommodated a living room, a dining room, four bedrooms, and staff quarters.

The sky-blue plumbago, long relieved of its climbing duties, grew and spread in the flower beds between one window and the next. The door was wide open; amidst the vine shoots of the chintz-covered couch slept a young man. A tall glass, still containing a bit of milk, stood on the floor next to a plate with two peach stones and a few bread crumbs.

"Hi there!" Lavinia said. The young man opened his eyes and smiled. He had dropped a folded sleeping bag and a knapsack on an armchair: obviously he was not a farm boy who had come to help straighten up the house and had fallen asleep on the job. The tennis shoes had left two dark traces on the couch. His eyes were blue, and his fine, soft, black hair exuded a silvery glow that made it look very light and almost transparent. His curls, not long enough to coil, looked like a halo of diaphanous question marks around the tall forehead.

"You must be Nicola's mother," the young man said, sitting up. "I was with him in the military service."

In that case, he was not so young. He must be at least Nicky's age, twenty-two, even if, like him, he had decided not to defer doing his civic duty to finish his studies.

"You're out of luck. My son is still in America."

"That's too bad." His smile disappeared, and his face expressed a heartfelt, almost childlike disappointment.

"I'm sorry," Lavinia said. And she really was. Several years earlier, as she was about to leave for Paris right on Christmas day, Nicola had looked at her with exactly the same expression on his face. It was odd how she had quite forgotten it until now. In fact, she hadn't paid much attention to it even when it had happened. Of course, she had thought, children always wanted to have everything right there and then: their mommy, their granny, their nanny, their dog, their teacher, the sea, the mountains, their friends, their teddy bear, the snow, the grass, TV, potato chips. But there were times when they could not. This is what she had thought then, while placing a kiss on that small, disappointed face, which she now believed she was seeing again, poor love.

"Do you need anything?" she asked him. "Are you hungry?"

The young man curled out of the sofa like a cat. He was not very tall, but his movements were those of a long-limbed person. "I have already helped myself. The fridge is full." He didn't apologize for his brazenness; instead, he asked her, "Would you like some coffee?"

"What? I'm not sure there is any."

"Yes, there is." He started walking toward the kitchen. "So, would you like some too?"

"Yes, thank you."

Lavinia followed him. Only now did she realize that she had walked through the garden very slowly, stopping here and there, wasting time, putting off as long as possible the moment when, after over twenty years, she would again cross the threshold of the Limonaia. She was afraid she might be assailed by memories so unbearable that she would, as usual, flee back under Violante's wing. But the young man's presence had changed her script, dispersing the shadows of the past, starting up a new chain of events and emotions.

There were flowers in the vases and bottles on the cart. Even in the kitchen, nothing was missing, and in the bathrooms there would certainly be the usual bars of soap, the same ones Violante had been buying for years by the case, from a very old factory that seemed to stay in operation only to supply her—and the bubble bath, the talcum powder, the toothpaste, all of them bearing the brand name of another venerable firm Violante alone knew and had patronized for almost half a century. Such comfort, such pleasure. A special attentiveness, as sweet as a caress, and as steady as a rock.

And now, smack in the middle of the picture, a new figure had appeared from a completely different species. A child who had come to play and eat a snack with his little friend.

"What's your name?" Lavinia asked him.

"Marco."

No last name. Maybe the use of a knapsack had replaced that of a last name. Lavinia felt the need to say something to plump up such a spare answer.

"I like Roman names. My name is Lavinia, also Roman."

Marco had filled the coffee maker with great dexterity. He must have been used to taking care of himself. "This house has been uninhabited for years," Lavinia added. "A few things may no longer work."

"Everything is fine in the kitchen," Marco answered. "The bathroom too seems to be OK." As soon as the coffee was ready, Marco placed the machine and all the other requisites—the sugar bowl, the milk jug, a white linen doily—on a silver tray; then he preceded Lavinia into the living room. He didn't speak much, but his silence didn't seem to bother him. Indeed, nothing seemed to bother him, not even the fact that Nicola wasn't there. Lavinia began to suspect she might have imagined the disappointment painted on his face. Had he rummaged through the entire house? He certainly behaved as if he was at home. . . . Maybe I should throw him out, Lavinia thought. But since she knew she wouldn't be able to do it, she said, "You hoped Nicola would be here, didn't you?" If he did not care, it was up to her to find a justification for that unexpected visit, and the impertinent ease with which he moved through the Limonaia. I should throw him out, she thought again. Otherwise she had to act as if everything were in order. "He is coming, of course, as usual, but a little later. School is over, but he has decided to spend a few weeks in New York—a friend has left him his apartment. You thought he was already here, didn't you?"

"Right."

They remained seated—she talking and he silent—until Violante showed up, followed by Nives and Margherita. Lavinia felt as if she had been caught red-handed in a compromising situation.

"This is Marco, a friend of Nicola's," she hastened to explain. "He was with him in the military." She couldn't have said when or how she had started noticing it, but she was aware of an underlying cockiness in Marco that went way beyond a mere excess of youthful casualness. In front of those three eminently respectable women, she felt ill at ease for having been his accomplice in refusing to put him in his place. She did not have the courage to tell them that she had found him peacefully installed in her house, and preferred to let them believe she had invited him.

9

I HAVE ASKED MY BARBER to come up to the Arnolfina to give me an impeccable shave. I have repeatedly noticed that women do not dislike hairy men, and that the excellence of a close shave seldom elicits from them the sort of admiration men expect. On the other hand, I have always behaved absurdly with Lavinia, like a silly Sisyphus who is doing his damnedest to be appreciated while knowing from the very start that his efforts will be in vain.

When I met her for the first time, she was a tall fifteen-year-old wearing a kilt, blue knee socks, and a disgruntled expression on her face which suggested that she was being dragged along against her will by her parents who did not know where to leave her, and were certainly old enough to be her grandparents. They wanted to sell me their last family treasures: two tempera paintings by Massimo d'Azeglio, a drawing by Ingres, and a wonderful battle scene which, with a bit of authority—such as I already had at twenty-eight—could easily have been palmed off as a work by Salvator Rosa.

Their exceedingly young daughter seemed to cause them more embarrassment than anything else. As if because of her, and very much against their will, they had been compelled to tarry on this earth beyond their natural date of extinction—a delay that explained the ashen color of their skin, and the vague smell of chrysanthemum and dust that enveloped them.

Next to them, Lavinia looked like an orphan, which, I think, was precisely what struck me from the very start, and made me ardently wish to take care of her. Though, in fact, that was not at all the way she herself looked, despite the long face and blue knee socks, but the way they made her look. In other words, I fell in love with something that was quite extraneous to her, emerging as it did out of her contiguity to those parents who looked like two exhausted players forced to put in extra innings on this earth.

Lavinia's hair was blond, fine, straight, brushed back and held in place by a tortoiseshell band. Her hairline was shaded: from the forehead and the temples, an almost imperceptible peach fuzz gradually turned into long threads of pale gold. It was the first time in my life that I had happened to notice someone's hairline, but I immediately realized how aristocratic that continuity between face, hair, and the surrounding air actually was. Casting a dismayed glance at the Venetian mirror above the console table in my waiting room, I felt uneasy and unusually unhappy about my physical appearance: I suddenly saw myself as someone wearing a brown mohair cap, a tawdry, insurmountable barrier against the dispersion and desirable blurring of the animal flesh and blood that constitute a face. My terrestrial brutality was there, perfectly visible and ineluctably confined within its dark boundaries. I felt as if I was all teeth, tongue, lips, nostrils . . . an indecent cluster of damp orifices in front of that adolescent who, instead, seemed to be evaporating upwardly, in a perpetual ascent.

From the vestibule, where I had met them, I led the way to my study. I held the door open for them to pass, but Lavinia shook her head and, with an almost imperceptible smile said, "I'm going to wait here." Clearly, in that family money was not a subject to be discussed in front of underage children; but I understood it a little too late, after I had already made the mistake of waving my arm and hinting at a triple welcome with my eyes.

I bought the paintings for a price that was far above their worth, only to realize immediately after that I had made another mistake, which, in their eyes, must have characterized me as little better than a gangster with a great deal of money but not enough culture to give a correct estimate of a work of art.

Five years later, when Lavinia, who by then really was an orphan, married Filippo, and, as a wedding present, I offered her precisely one of those paintings—the battle scene which I had never resold—I again had the feeling I had done something terribly wrong, a feeling that made me break into a cold sweat at the very moment when, according to my calculations, the delivery man must have reached the door of the squalid apartment that Lavinia was about to leave forever.

Only when it was too late to back off did I realize that the value of my present was vulgarly excessive, and that its choice was irreparably inappropriate. I had meant it as a kindness, true, but it was an awkward, inopportune kindness . . . in short, I duly lashed myself for it.

Lavinia's reaction to that sensational present was very gracious, if sibylline: she thanked me with a very affectionate letter, but she never gave me any indication of having recognized the painting—and I still don't know whether it was because she had quite forgotten it, or because she did not want to acknowledge the awkwardness of my gesture.

So it is without faith, but conscientiously, that I have let myself be shaved, refreshed, and massaged, and have decked myself out in an expensive white linen suit to attend Violante Santini's dinner. The fact that Lavinia is staying at the Limonaia might well be a point in my favor since it could alter the usual course of events, if nothing else by providing a different setting for our first meeting.

Fortunately, the shortest way to reach Violante's villa from the Arnolfina leads into the park through a small secondary gate, and borders the patio of the Limonaia. I am so shy with Lavinia, even in the silliest matters, that I relish the opportunity of walking by her house pretending—only with myself since there is nobody else in sight—that I have only just realized that the Limonaia is open and inhabited. As I am crossing the stone patio, I slow down, then, assuming an expression of pleasant surprise, I stop. "Lavinia!" I exclaim. I walk up to the door and pull the bronze bell. "Anybody home?"

Her voice answers me from within. "Is it you, Aldo? Come in, I'll be right there."

As I walk in, she briefly appears at the other end of the room, beyond the open door leading to the bedrooms. She is barefoot, and, with her elbows raised above her head, is reaching behind her back to zip up her dress.

"Coming." She disappears, while her voice, now muffled, tells me about the weather in Milan, and the awful trip: the sort of thing one talks about when meeting again after an absence. There is something conjugal to the scene: I, all dressed up and waiting for her in the living room, and she, almost, but not quite, ready to go out, speaking to each other through a wall.

I feel a pang of regret for not having condescended to marry one of the young women—quite a few—who would have been glad to have me; while she goes on talking, I think of the daily gestures of couples, their expressions of love, their closeness, and for a moment am sure that any marriage would have been better than none.

"Are you coming to Violante's?" Lavinia shouts.

"Yes, I am."

"Well, then we can go together. Pour yourself something to drink."

She reappears wearing shoes and carrying a sweater and handbag.

Seeing her in full light is enough to rekindle my feeling—

whether madness or obsession: that disease which I have nurtured for almost thirty years—and let it burn, if not with the roar and ravenous flames of times past, with a slow but steady and lasting fire. No, no other woman could have given me anything worth regretting.

She pecks me on the cheek as she hastens to the front door and leans out. "Sigmund!" she shouts. "Pour me a drop too," she goes on without turning, still apparently addressing the park and the dog barking in the distance. "Everything you need is there. When I got here, that house looked as if it had never been closed up. Violante is phenomenal, and Nives too. Come, schatzerle, you can't carry on like that all the time."

Sigmund bursts into the room like a shot, leaps up onto the sofa then down again, and starts careening through the room, crumpling the rugs, his tongue hanging out, his ears thrown back, his mouth wide open on an ecstatic smile.

"This is too much!" Lavinia cries out with a plaintive voice suggesting weary distress, and the bewildered—maybe a little shortsighted—look of one who has just forgotten something and is about to lose something else in an uninterrupted chain of minor catastrophes caused by aristocratic ineptitude—very Myrna Loy, very thirties, including the dog and the dress, loosely draped on her slim figure in elegantly démodé folds. "Das ist ganz ausgeschlossen!" She often speaks German to the dog. "Enough, dearest. Margherita, help! Come get this devil and put him to bed."

The maid appears, grabs the dog, places him under her arm, straightens the rugs out with the tip of her shoe, and then withdraws. The balmy evening air suddenly fills the room like a rippleless lake. Lavinia slumps into an armchair.

"Sigmund is so happy in the country that I'm always afraid he might die of a heart attack."

I pick up the conversation where we left off. "You were telling me about your trip."

"Horrible, dreadfully hot."

"And what about you, in Milan?"

"A disaster. My much-esteemed sociologist is addicted to infidelity, neither more or less than if he were a drunk or a junkie. He can't do without it, nor does he care where he gets it."

Now, I know, we'll be able to talk calmly, without interruptions. Lavinia can devote herself entirely to her interlocutor only when speaking of her love life; otherwise, any conversation with her is doomed to crumble into innumerable fragments, none of which will ever reach a conclusion, being inevitably interrupted by the next one, and so on and so forth to exhaustion. In part, it is Lavinia who constantly interrupts herself to scold the dog, call Margherita, go look for cigarettes; and in part it is the exterior world that seems magically provoked into interrupting her: the phone, the Mormon with his leaflets, and, on one occasion, in Milan, even an earthquake, as if she had ordered its delivery just in time to protect the randomness of our conversation.

But her favorite subject is her love life, and when she gets going, nothing can distract her. She talks about it with me, with Violante, with Cynthia and Leopoldo, not to mention her official psychoanalyst and all the auxiliary ones, her innumerable Milanese friends who share the same privilege.

She does not do it because she needs to get it off her chest, or wants to see things a little bit more clearly, or, least of all, because she seeks advice. Besides, she already knows what I would tell her: get rid of that jerk (and the previous one, and the next one) and love me.

But this is not what she wants: she wants to speak of her beloved, and utter his name as often possible to have the illusion he is nearby, caught in a relentless web of words, bound to her by an endless verbal leash.

"He is desperately scared of death, you see, and infidelity— that is to say, duplicity—provides him with an alter ego, a second chance, a being elsewhere . . ."

Predictably, she drowns me in psychobabble. And, as usual, I feel an irrepressible urge to bring her back to earth with the crassest common sense, because if it is true that I have loved this woman for almost thirty years, it is also true that no one in the world can irritate me as much as she.

"If you like him," I tell her, "keep him as he is; otherwise get rid of him. If you want to know my opinion, I think you should do the latter."

"Oh! You think it's easy!" she sighs with a dejected smile.

"It's the easiest thing in this world. I don't believe in this constant need to analyze people—yourself as well as others. I don't think it's healthy, in fact I am sure it is bad."

"Violante told me the same thing this afternoon."

"It doesn't surprise me. She is a very wise woman."

"I know, dear, you are wise too. But this is a different game. . . . You, she, and all the people around you, in this part of the world, you live in a universe that has never been touched by psychoanalysis: a sort of national park full of deer and antelopes in their natural state. You speak a different language and think differently. Believe me, things are much more complex than they seem to you."

She looks at me affectionately; her eyes are full of melancholy wisdom. Maybe she is expecting me to jump from one piece of furniture to the next to confirm my true nature as a protected species.

I glance at my watch. "We are late," I tell her. It is not true, but I like to be on time, and I know Lavinia.

"I must change," she sighs. "Let me finish my Scotch and I'll go."

"But you have just changed. You were putting that dress on when I arrived. You are beautiful as you are."

She slips off her sandals, draws up her long, slim legs, and cuddles on the sofa like a fluid spiral, a wisteria shoot, too tenuous not to bow under its own weight.

"Esther Williams will be wrapped in a fuchsia satin gown and a pastel mink stole. I must keep up with the Joneses."

Like a schoolboy, I'd like to kneel at her feet and tell her 'I love you.' Instead, I say, "I like Cynthia. I even find her elegant in her Columbus, Ohio way. As for you, my dear, you are a snob."

This time she breaks into a genuine smile. "But I like her too, you know. My snootiness means nothing." Her smile grows larger. "I'm sure she does the same thing with me. I guess there is some mutual rivalry."

"Over what?"

"Oh, I don't know. Violante's love. Primogeniture: she is the wife of the current head of the family and I am the older son's widow. . . . All this sounds terribly outdated, but it isn't, not here, as you well know."

"You hold the winning hand: you are the heir's mother."

"That's true."

In the end, she does not change her dress. It was just a pretext to delay things, a habit of hers, and above all, to bring the talk back to Sandro. We arrive at Violante's late: I, terribly embarrassed; she, as if it were nothing.

10

THE TABLE IS SET under the dog rose pergola; a little further back, the Mauritian servant is passing around crackers and white wine to the guests seated around Violante in a crown of easy chairs. Besides Cynthia and Leopoldo, there are two American sculptors, husband and wife, representing the local Anglo-Saxon colony; Violante's Milanese publisher (she writes cookbooks); and Nicola's friend, the young man I spoke to earlier this morning. At Violante's, symmetry reigns supreme over even the smallest family dinners; I suppose the publisher was invited to reach a perfect balance between ladies and gentlemen, which has now again been thrown out of kilter by the unexpected arrival of the ephebe. The conversation seems to revolve around the particular qualities of cities throughout the world; but to judge from the last, weary exchanges, the interest must be flagging.

"Then, of course, there is Zurich," the American sculptress concludes.

"Zurich? Why Zurich?" the publisher inquires. "There are hundreds of cities in the world I like better than Zurich."

"But it is so reassuring. To us, I mean, to all those who live here. One has to have one's teeth cleaned now and then, don't you think?"

The ephebe's light blue eyes glower at the sculptress, his red lips already gathered in a pout. I wonder whether he is shocked by the woman's tactlessness or simply bored because he doesn't know English and therefore cannot understand what she is saying. It is Cynthia who comes to the rescue of her adoptive country.

"My dear, I really don't think you have to go as far as Zurich to have your teeth cleaned. Here they already had dentists when the Zurichers—not to mention our own ancestors—were still walking on all fours."

Violante catches the eyes of the Mauritian servant and stands up. "Let's have dinner," she says. "Our cuisine is even better than our dentists."

"I didn't get your name," I tell the young man as we walk toward the pergola. The crickets are chirring, the gravel crunches under our steps.

"Marco," the young man answers.

"Where did you meet Nicola?"

"In the military." His hair is slightly wet.

"You've gone for a swim in the pool?" I ask him.

"Yes."

He's not much help. His monosyllables plop like drops of opaque liquid among the evening sounds. Without regret, I leave him to his silence, glad that the seating arrangement spares me from having to entertain him.

Violante sits at the head of the table and I at her left, followed by the sculptress, Leopoldo, and finally Marco. The sculptor is sitting in front of me, with Lavinia on his right, then the sculptor and, last, Cynthia. A bowl of sweet peas is replacing the missing guest at the other end of the table, opposite Violante. Marco's beauty and youth are like Hermaphroditus's and find an apt symmetrical reflection in Cynthia's plump and tender femininity.

The conversation continues in English.

"I'm afraid your young guest doesn't understand a single word," I whisper in Violante's ear.

"I don't know. He pulls the same face even when you speak to him in Italian. He doesn't seem to be willing to do anything harder than just sit there and look young. He is not like our Nicola. You know," she went on without pausing, "I may need your help." Maybe she wants to buy or sell a painting. "Nives is awfully smart and full of common sense," she goes on, "but I don't think I can count on her in this particular instance."

Nives? Obviously it has nothing to do with a painting.

"I am at your disposal," I assure her.

"Thank you. At first you might find my project somewhat abstract, but you'll soon realize that it's the right way."

I try to make her tell me what it is all about, but to no avail. "This is not the right moment," she says and, looking around the table, changes the subject. "Look at that boy. Who would have ever thought that he would be the life of the party?"

By and by, the quiet little idol has become the center of attention. Everybody—except Violante and myself—is paying court to him with courtesies, witticisms, and all sorts of worldly charm. They are no longer speaking English, now; even the two American sculptors struggle with an Italian that twenty-some years among us have done little to improve. They are all as excited as children who have just been given a puppy, while Marco—just like a sleepy, indifferent puppy who submits to the games and caresses of his young new masters—sits quietly in front of his plate, a hint of a smile barely curling the corners of his mouth, his light eyes shifting from one interlocutor to the next with a look of utter aloofness.

After dinner, Cynthia gives him a tour of the library, and later, Leopoldo takes him to the cellar to look for a bottle of white wine. Around midnight, I ask Violante, "Where is our little prince sleeping tonight?"

She looks surprised. "In his own home, I suppose. Why?"

"Because I don't think he lives around here. This morning I met him while he was walking up the road with a knapsack on his back. His home must be elsewhere. Someone will have to offer him a bed."

"Well, . . ." she says. She tilts her head slightly to the side while her birdlike pupils dilate as if at the sight of some juicy worm. "He is a friend of Nicola's: Lavinia will have to take care of him."

This is new. As a rule, whatever concerns Nicola is Violante's province; in the very rare instances when there is some obstacle—as when she was ill—the task is passed on to Lavinia, Nives, or Cynthia, indifferently, depending on which of the three is most available at the moment—something Lavinia seldom is. On those occasions, the person in charge acts exclusively as Violante's representative. I have never heard my old friend abdicate—even if only in words—her guardianship of her grandson.

I gaze at her perplexed, wondering whether I should consider the sentence as a declaration of her future plans, and whether—in this case—I should express my opinion in favor of Lavinia, if nothing else with some fairly banal remark—the only one that crosses my mind—concerning the fact that, after all, she is the boy's mother.

I say it. "After all, your daughter-in-law is Nicola's mother. She'll take care of it."

From the very day the child was born, I have always had great difficulty defending Lavinia's maternal rights, partly because she has always seemed very, very far from wishing such a thing. Set side by side, the bed where she lay after having given birth and the white cradle of her child seemed to contain two equally defenseless creatures, more than willing to let the efficient lady in the pastel linen suit nourish, clean, and generally take care of them according to an extremely clear and comprehensive plan—hospital file, feeding schedule, and two weight charts, the first marking Nicola's progressive growth and the second, Lavinia's gradual return to her former self.

A few years later, the young mother found a small apartment in Milan (via Cappuccio) and a nice job at Olivetti; while the child, barely out of kindergarten, was secured a very costly, if precautionary, place at Harvard.

The child's bedroom, on via Cappuccio, was soon devoted to other uses. The day Lavinia first crossed her legs behind her new desk at Olivetti—two weeks before the opening of the Scala—Nicola, in a white frock with a blue bow, was sitting at a school bench some two hundred miles away. It had been decided that he would stay in Tuscany with his grandmother since his mommy, in her new role as career girl, wouldn't have the time to enjoy his company during the week. She would, however, bravely join the general weekend exodus to go spend Saturday and Sunday with him.

During the previous six years, in Lucca, Lavinia had tried other options: the university, a boutique, painting. She and the child lived at Villa Grande. The Limonaia was saturated with sad memories and, anyway, it seemed a useless hassle to have to reopen it when Nicky was so comfortably settled in the bedroom next to his grandmother's, and Lavinia in two handsome rooms with bathroom on the second floor—rooms that seemed particularly right during her artistic period, as they both faced north.

The job at Olivetti was followed by a rare-book store, which Lavinia had opened with a friend. Meanwhile, the child was growing up in the balmy country air—it would have been madness to move him to the noxious fogs of Lombardy; besides, Lavinia's supersmart and centrally located little bookshop took up so much of her time that she would have never been able to take care of Nicola as well as his grandmother.

Soon enough it was time to think of high school: Lucca's *liceo classico* had been, and probably still was, one of the very best in the world, a breeding ground for politicians, philosophers, writers, artists. Nicola was much better off where he was.

Then he went through military service. "No exemption. You'll do like everybody else," Violante had decided. And now he is in an American college. Nicola's bedroom on via Cappuccio has long been used as a wardrobe; when he goes to visit his mother in Milan, he sleeps on the sofa, in the living room.

I said the only thing I could say. I repeat it: "Lavinia should take care of it."

Violante casts a rapid glance across the room, where Marco is still quietly weaving his spell. "The more I look at him the less I like him. I doubt he is really Nicola's friend. Though," she adds, "he is all too easy to please. You have no idea what kind of boors he has brought home."

"He has a soft spot for strays of all sorts, whether animal or human."

"True. One would think all the dogs and cats of the area had heard about him. Even when Nicola is away, there isn't a single lost and hungry fleabag within a radius of I don't know how many miles that won't show up at my door expecting—and with reason—to be welcome."

Marco is now sitting in an armchair next to the empty fireplace, his ankles crossed, his hands clasped in his lap, his head erect, his eyes serene. Cynthia and the publisher are involved in a lively conversation, but rather than addressing each other they seem to be addressing him, like two court actors reciting a dialogue for the amusement of the heir apparent.

"I'm afraid," Violante continues, "this little angel might have something similar in mind."

"You mean, to be adopted as a house pet?"

"To spend his holidays with us. To settle in, while waiting for Nicola. He is not a dog or a cat. Humans are much more dangerous. What do we know but that he is here with the intention of killing us all in our sleep and taking off with the silver in his knapsack?"

"You really don't like him," I observe.

"Not a bit. He makes me uncomfortable. Look at him. He sits there like someone who has decided that no amount of torture is going to pull his secret out of him."

"Or someone who's trying not to show the profound disgust he can't help feeling."

"Right. He sits there and watches. It is inhuman to conceal one's thoughts so thoroughly. Unless, of course, he doesn't think. Maybe he is sleeping with his eyes open."

Lavinia approaches us, bends over Violante, and kisses her on the cheek. "I'd better go. I'm very tired, and I still have to make Marco's bed."

Cynthia has also stood up and, grabbing the boy's hand, has pulled him out of his armchair.

"Up you go!" She takes him by the arm and drags him after her sister-in-law.

"We are all leaving. I can prepare his bed if you are too tired. Marco, would you mind staying at my place?"

"Whatever," the boy answers.

We take our leave of Violante and walk out. In the distance, a light is visible at one of the Limonaia's windows.

"I am not that tired," Lavinia says. "Besides, it looks as if Margherita is still up. Don't worry, Cynthia, Marco is staying at my place."

"OK."

I've the feeling that a small battle has just been fought and Lavinia has won it. Or am I imagining things? What could have happened during the evening to justify my taking the indefinable excitement I have sensed in the air seriously, and interpreting it as the surface reflection of a subterranean struggle among the adults to attract the youth's attention?

In fact, nothing has happened. Violante and I were sitting to the side and could only hear the others' voices without distinguishing any of their words. As we say good-bye to the American sculptors and the publisher, and watch their cars drive away down the gravel path, I almost convince myself that I imagined everything.

Lavinia, Cynthia, and the others, I tell myself, were only involved in a lively conversation, as is normal in society; as for the boy, he looked so Olympian and expressionless not because he was at the center of some sort of pagan rite in honor of youth and beauty but simply because he was bored and was in fact sleeping with his eyes open, as Violante suggested. Lavinia's and Cynthia's exchange was a courtesy contest, not a midsummer conflict over the graces of a pageboy.

We all walk toward our respective homes, the boy in front between Cynthia and Leopoldo, Lavinia and I a few steps behind them. In the middle of the sky, the moon is a white as chalk; we are steeped in a silvery light that seems to emanate from the garden with the scent of the flowers rather than coming down from above.

Lavinia tears off a shoot of honeysuckle, passes it under her nose absentmindedly, and then starts crushing it with her fingers.

"I envy those who have no emotions, and are able to arouse them in others without feeling anything themselves," she sighs. The tone in her voice is at once pained and elegant—but, as usual, more elegant than pained—and I again wonder, as I have for a lifetime, whether one should trust a sorrow that's expressed with such distinction.

"We don't know him well enough," I answer. "Maybe he seems so impermeable because he is shy."

Marco is walking lightly ahead of us; the two figures at his sides look heavy and dense in comparison. "How can we possibly judge someone like him?" I continue. "We don't even know what he does, all we know is that he wears tennis shoes, sleeps in a sleeping bag, and turns to strangers for a meal and a place to stay. He belongs to a different race. We have no terms of comparison for someone like him."

"Oh, him. Actually, I was referring to Sandro." To hear that

Lavinia's thoughts have been, as usual, converging on her unfaithful sociologist comes as such a relief to me that I can't help but acknowledge the fact that throughout the entire evening I have been jealous of Marco.

"Oh, him," I echo her nonchalantly. Better a lion in the Sahara desert than a flea in my bed, or, more to the point, better a charming sociologist in the middle of the Aegean sea than a petty seducer in the guest room at the Limonaia.

"Yes, him," she giggles nervously. "I can't think of anything else, believe me. And that is precisely what infuriates him. I can't help whining and being suffocating. A fatal tactical error. And I always feel it coming, you see, as if it were an approaching storm I can do nothing to stop. Careful, I tell myself, you are about to do something very stupid. And so I do, without fail. And all the while I can see myself, in total clarity. I look horrible: my face sags, I get pimples, a bellyache, bags under my eyes . . . you can't even imagine what I look like."

I refrain from letting her know what I think: that no man deserves as much suffering, least of all Sandro, the sociologist—an unbearable quack who puckers his lips and casts bewitching glances like a silent movie star. Nor do I cite myself as an example to follow, as I could: 'I also know the pain of unrequited love, for you, but I do not let it destroy me.' Instead, I put my arm around her shoulders, gently draw her toward me, and place a chaste kiss on her temple.

We greet Leopoldo and Cynthia, who turn away in the direction of their own house. After a few more steps we reach the patio in front of the Limonaia. Margherita has already gone to sleep; the light we saw from Violante's pergola is the one we forgot to switch off in the living room before leaving. We stop in the large yellow arcade reflected onto the gray stones of the patio.

"Would you like something to drink?" Lavinia inquires.

I decline. Marco sits on a wicker chair. "I would like an orange juice," he answers.

"I don't know if there is any."

"Yes, there is. I saw it in the fridge. In the lowest door shelf, with the other bottles."

Lavinia gives me a kiss. "If you don't want anything to drink, I'll let you go to bed." She pushes me toward the dark path that leads up to the Arnolfina and hurries into her house to get the orange juice. The back of the wicker chair in which Marco is sitting fans out into a series of whorls that look like a sort of wide, golden filigree halo surrounding his head. He sits there, not sprawling all over as most boys would, but enigmatically, almost orientally, composed.

He has settled in that chair like some god, and is now waiting to be served; I bet he won't even get up to help Lavinia make his bed.

From the deep shadow of the trees into which I am about to disappear, I turn one last time to steal a glance at him and am seized by an ever-growing, and now more than reasonable irritation.

I once stayed at Lavinia's in Milan, on my way back from Amsterdam. I had forgotten to reserve a hotel room and arrived in the middle of a fashion fair that had filled the center of the city with Japanese buyers. The Germans and the Americans had found lodgings in the adjoining areas, followed, along a series of concentric circles, by the other various ethnic groups in a decreasing order of efficiency and foresight, with the French and the Spaniards last, in the area around Bergamo, and last of all, myself, out in the streets.

It was a Thursday evening, Margherita's day off. Lavinia had welcomed me very warmly—I even imagined that she had not gone out in order to be there when I arrived—but when it was time to go to bed, she showed me how to open the sofa bed, handed me a pile of immaculate sheets, pillow cases, and blankets, and then withdrew to her room. Inwardly, I immediately decided that that was exactly how it should be, and that I was happy that way, though I had secretly wished to see her fuss over me like a mother hen.

We were both traditionally unfit to consider domestic chores as falling within our sphere of competence: I as a man, and she as a member of the upper class. In my milieu, women made beds; in hers, servants. So, if one of us had to adjust, why shouldn't I be the one since, after all, it was my bed that was in question?

As I reach the top of my tower, I do not switch on the light. Instead, I lean out of the window overlooking the Limonaia with my navy binoculars. I'm stirred by jealousy and a sense of deep injustice, along with an overwhelming need to know, and to watch. I am sure Lavinia will make that rascal's bed, and I want to witness the entire scene.

Up there, away from everybody, cloaked in my own voyeuristic darkness, so far from them and yet so close thanks to my lenses' magnifying power, I am, still and again, a thirteen-year-old boy lulled by the scent of gardenias and the music of mellow voices and tinkling crystal—the brush, like an angel's kiss, between a porcelain cup and a silver teaspoon—but also, as if forty years had elapsed in a second—a middle-aged man rich with money and success, perched like an old crow on the stones of a tower, surviving on the same ancient and unrequited love.

There he is, in his wicker shrine, with a glass of orange juice in his hand, while Lavinia, whom I can see perfectly through the open French window, is fluttering around his bed, spreading out a sheet, shaking it in the air, tucking it around the mattress, smoothing it out with her hands. Sigmund keeps coming and going as if busy conveying messages between his mistress and the boy sitting in a wicker chair on the patio.

The bed has been made, and now Lavinia, a glass in her hand, steps out of the house to go sit next to Marco. I don't think I would hear them if they were talking, but they seem to be silent. Indeed, they seem to be suspended in a pause, as if the author of the unfolding story had stopped writing to wonder what to say next. All the possible continuations hover around their heads like ghosts, "things" beyond words, primordial, not created by men through language.

Later, when one of the ghosts has shooed away all the others and assumed a concrete form, turning from hypothesis into fact, then, calmly, I will be able to tuck everything back into the Procustean bed of signs, and recover the certainty that there is nothing beyond words, and that the threatening shadow I see from the corner of my eye is only bad digestion.

11

R EPLACE WALNUT SECRETARY w. directoire bureau in tulip room; bring wal. sec. to pol.; fix ext. leg on oval dinner table.

Violante closed the notebook and placed it on the nighttable with the pen. Those were all marginal details in the grandiose plan on which she was currently working and to which she would return the following morning, but not while in bed. Some sort of very intricate blueprint was gradually taking shape on the large sheet of drawing paper she had tacked to her worktable.

Luckily, she did not have to write a will, which simplified things considerably. Succession laws were wise, and her heirs—Leopoldo and Nicola—were both legitimate and full of reciprocal devotion. Besides, she had very little to bequeath. Nothing on the side of her own family—her father had been a penniless music teacher, and her husband had died before the passage of the law granting the status of heir to the surviving spouse. She almost forgot her only real possession—the literary estate consisting of nine published cookbooks—as if it were of no account, something silly, like the gold tinfoil medal earned at Sunday school, or the bouquets of violets from an unexpected admirer. And yet, every six months, her books, and particularly the last one—*Wheat, Corn, and Spelt in Mediterranean Cuisine,* translated into several languages—brought in a royalty check whose amount varied but was always more than what she expected. Violante's mind complacently lingered—but just for a second— on her writing activity; then skimmed over *The French Cook's Recipe Book* by Elisa Baciocchi, which she had found in some archive and whose publication she meant to undertake—if she had the time. Then, she dutifully returned to the tangle she had the sacred obligation to unravel before it was too late, straightening out each stem in its ideal direction, not going against nature but rather lending it a hand in avoiding dead ends and useless turns, so that everything might continue growing in a satisfactory manner.

It was a grandiose plan. Even the furniture to be polished and the plants to be replaced in the garden were part of it, minor expressions of the general equilibrium. At its center were the relationship between Leopoldo and Cynthia—including the child that should be born within the next three years, at most— and Lavinia's emotional stability. At the center of the center, however, was Nicola, who had to be given back to the person who had physically given him birth, not so much to provide him with a mother—at twenty-two they are no longer necessary—as to provide Lavinia with a son, at last. But though these were the essential points, the true grandiosity of the plan—of which she herself at times, almost overwhelmed, lost sight—lay in the simultaneous presence and mutual interdependence of so many heterogeneous elements that were so tightly bound together by their own ineluctable gravitational law that nothing, not the slightest thing, could be neglected: the gardener's retirement plan, the distribution of the three houses so that their recipients would find themselves in the place best suited to their roles, a complete overhauling of Villa Grande's heating system, and, of course, Nives's employment after Violante's death, since almost everything depended on that.

On the other hand, she had absolutely no power over Nives's decisions: at least not directly, since she could not acquaint her with her plan or convince her to accept it. Nives always refused to go along with her in the geometry of her programs: Violante had known this for a long time and no longer tried to involve her in them. "My dear madam," she would have told her, "this is not like gardening—seeding, uprooting, transplanting, fertilizing, all the while knowing that the results will somehow correspond to our expectations! This is not a flower bed, this involves people's lives!"

She could confide in Nives—as she had done for years—as long as she was unable to see things clearly; but the moment she had all the elements in hand, and started working with them as if she had a geometry problem to solve, she had better go at it on her own. Nives disapproved of strategies. She thought it more human, and maybe even more moral, to play it by ear, trusting equally one's good will, the mood of the moment, fantasy. "We'll do our best," she would say. "If they are roses, they will bloom."

What would she have said had she known that the two curves that lightly grazed each other in the complex diagram tacked on Violante's desk represented Lavinia and Nicola, and that if everything worked out according to Violante's plans and the two figures came in direct contact with each other it would mean that she had succeeded in tearing a son out of her heart to return him to the woman who had given him birth? Could Nives accept the idea that such a cataclysm could be planned by drawing curves on a sheet of paper?

Violante clasped her hands on her chest and closed her eyes. How much time did she have left? She did not mean how many more years to live: true, she had already felt death's first stirrings within her, but she knew it could go on for a very long time. It had not taken some new infirmity to prod her on to put her things in order, but rather a sudden opening up of her awareness that one day she would also die, like everybody else. She was as fit as a fiddle and could go on for ten, maybe even twenty more years.

It was the others' opportunities that were wearing out, and then it would be too late. She couldn't just sit and wait for her own death, and let them fend for themselves. She had reigned too long and too well to simply up and leave.

What did they know? How much did they understand? They thought she ordered the soap and the toilet paper, bought wedding presents for her tenant farmers' children, took care of the garden, called the plumber, the upholsterer . . . they saw her do each of these things, and many others besides, but always one by one, separately, without ever realizing that all of them taken together—and what's more with an extraordinary sense of duty, as if they were all her responsibility—meant "to reign." They couldn't even imagine—and Nives, who could, did not want to—that if another queen was not there ready to take over when she was gone, everything would disintegrate in less than a year. Each of them would grab his or her favorite morsel and hide away to eat it in watchful solitude; and the barbarity . . . Why on earth had she come up with such a big word?

Indeed, what would happen if one day there was no longer anyone who knew how many *panettoni* to buy for Christmas? What relationship was there between the survival of civilization and the certainty that every Christmas for as long as they lived the parish priest, the two tenant farmers, the gardener, and all the others, including Bruna, the visiting nurse, would keep receiving the same semicircular cardboard box with the picture of the Milan cathedral? How could a panettone, itself a product of lemming logic, stave off the senseless accumulation of waste, the mad flight of a present without memory and without hopes—and what use was the little reserve of good will and good education accumulated during her reign, if . . .

The subject and the predicate kept moving farther and farther apart until they almost lost sight of each other across a sea of words, words, words . . . it meant that she was falling asleep. The mere thought of it woke her up.

What they needed was a national park, a sanctuary, a circumscribed, well-protected area within which no law would be allowed that said that novelty is in itself a value; a small territory that wouldn't be strewn daily with the refuse of the previous day and recklessly suffocated under heaps of cadavers—the putrefying carcasses of ideas, songs, characters, books, all the things that kept being dished out in haste and sloppiness to be trashed the next day.

It had been much simpler for her husband to leave the paper mill, itself an ancient kingdom that had belonged to the same family for three hundred years. And yet, Filippo, the designated heir, had risked spoiling everything by dying three years before his own father. He was to manage the mill when the time came, while Leopoldo, who was still only a boy—there was a difference of fifteen years between the two brothers—would have to spend a number of years learning the ropes under his older brother's supervision.

Instead, oddly enough, Filippo's sudden disappearance from his post in the firm had gone practically unnoticed. Everything had immediately adjusted to his absence. Leopoldo had returned from Canada, where he had been sent for a period of training in the cellulose plant of one of their oldest suppliers, and had effortlessly taken on all the responsibilities that had once fallen on his brother—including the chess game with his father every Monday evening.

Then he had married Cynthia, and when, only three years later, the reins of the business had been passed to him, he had straight off done an excellent job. His wife's dollars had certainly helped him survive the crisis which had affected that entire economic sector in those years, but they had not been crucial.

And yet, the paper mill—that allied kingdom in which Violante had never dared poke her nose but which she had watched prosper for years right next door—seemed so vast and difficult to govern . . . ceaselessly fermenting, teeming with workers, employers, clients suppliers, unions, banks, laws, plants. But of course, each of them knew what his function was—it was even spelled out in the contract—and that was a big advantage. The brief three years between his brother's mad flight and his father's death had actually been enough for Leopoldo to get ready to wear the crown.

Lavinia, on the other hand, didn't even know there was a crown to wear. If there was no time for Violante to change things, she would let it roll into a ditch as if it were an empty can of tomatoes.

Suddenly, Violante became aware of the smell of goats and oriental spices; she heard the call of a muezzin. The water that ran in the middle of the road dragged the crown away, tossing it right and left on the paving stones with a dismal clatter.

Violante let go, and glided slowly into sleep.

12

CYNTHIA TURNED OFF THE LIGHT in the entrance hall and
started walking upstairs. Once home, while Leopoldo was bolt-
ing the front door, instead of proceeding immediately to her
bedroom she had stopped in the library. There she had kicked
off her sandals and had cuddled up on the red velvet sofa,
tucking her legs under her body, closing in upon herself, she
thought, like a tender little pet that can be picked up in the palm
of one hand and stroked on its tiny head with a big, gentle index
finger. That moment could have been the finest of the day: the
two of them, alone, he would have brought her a glass of milk
and would have sat next to her, repeating the words and gestures of their engagement days and the first months of their
marriage—she still missed those times, while he had forgotten
them who knows where, at the bottom of his memory. Instead,
Leopoldo had quickly peeked into the room to wish her good
night, and had gone upstairs, where each of them had a personal
bedroom and bathroom, two separate planets whose orbits
never crossed.

On the other hand, she had married Leopoldo precisely because she had understood that he would be able to "respect"

her, a verb she had first learned when she was sixteen, during her grand tour of Italy, from an old maid at the Villa Silvestri pensione in Florence. Cynthia was happy to have a chance to practice her Italian, and poor Dilva wanted nothing better than to tell her about that extraordinary young man—a handsome, distinguished accountant—who showered her with attention and yet knew how to "respect" her. "I wonder what he sees in me," she would sigh with a blissful smile. Only when the handsome accountant disappeared with all the jewels and money from the pensione's safe did one understand what lay behind all his attentions and respect of poor Dilva.

But, of course, to Leopoldo "respect" meant something different. It meant that he intuited—without her having to defend herself—the precise point where, for Cynthia, physical contact turned from sweet intimacy into something nauseating that she was utterly unable to bear. Though they had never explicitly agreed on it—the mere mention of it revolted her—Cynthia had always been sure that even after their wedding he would not dare impose such a disgusting violence upon her; and since he "respected" her, he wouldn't force her to reject him, knowing that even that would make her die with shame, as it would clearly acknowledge that there had been a request, and before it, a sickening desire.

Before meeting Leopoldo, she had already been in love, and therefore knew the feeling and how it evolved, from beginning to end. At first, there was the sweetest emotion, as if the heart were about to overflow with tears of tenderness—a nearly unbearable happiness. Then, suddenly, everything degenerated into a disagreable confrontation: the face of the beloved became a bestial mask hovering over her—each dilated pore in the foreground—while the moist, animal warmth of his breath enveloped her hair and face in a viscous web . . .

The first time, millions of years ago—he was a schoolmate, and his name was Buddy—she had screamed, had run out of the car, parked right behind the ballpark, and had vomited right on the edge of the road. Then, she had kept on running, nonstop—she had even lost her shoes—until, filthy, her stockings tattered, she had locked herself up in her dorm room. She had stood under the shower for hours, unable to stop washing. Later, Marjorie, her roommate, had pulled her out, dried her off, comforted her, tucked her in bed.

Afterward, she had been able to organize her love life the way she wanted it, enjoying the part that she liked for as long as it lasted: the sweet, sweet languor, the soulful sighs, the skipped heartbeats and furtive kisses, the accidental grazing of hands, her head resting on his shoulder—that lovely vale of tenderness through which one could hear the other's life flow, like the sea in a conch.

That was as much physical closeness as any man could expect from Cynthia Timmis. She had learned how to prolong that moment of supreme happiness and how to recognize the warning signs of the horrible metamorphosis; that's when she fled, full of disgust and regret. The object of both feelings was the same man, except that, to her, it was as if an axe had dropped from the sky and divided him into two different persons: a dead beloved and a living beast oozing animal humors, eager to contaminate her with his own turpitude.

Then she had met Leopoldo—as ancient, refined, and weary as the Europe he seemed to incarnate—endowed with a surprising sensitivity that could only be compared to the subtlest musical ear. He might, in the distant future, offend her, or deliberately wound her—Cynthia sensed this immediately, indeed, she foresaw it as if a sudden flash of clairvoyance had torn the amorous mist that enveloped her—but would never, ever, disgust her with unintentional coarseness.

So, she had loved him without fear, knowing that he would never do anything to break the spell: neither intentionally, because he loved her and did not want to lose her, nor by mistake, because he did not make that sort of mistake.

During the very short engagement, Leopoldo may have

thought that Cynthia was only a staunch puritan and that, after the wedding—as soon as the thing was officially sanctioned by law—she would willingly submit to that infamy: it was possible, but she had quickly dispelled even this last doubt by refusing to linger on it.

To marry him without first putting all her cards on the table wouldn't have been fair, and to behave unfairly would have been like reneging on a deeply ingrained tradition, something that was hers by birth, like a Thanksgiving turkey with chestnut stuffing. On the other hand, she couldn't give up Leopoldo—since she had first laid her eyes on him she had been in love as never before and the mere idea of losing him panicked her.

After the wedding, when he had understood—the slightest trifle had been enough for him to understand—nothing dramatic had happened, at least not outwardly. He had gone on loving her—indeed, more than ever—and she had adored him. She had thought that everything was marvelous and that there was absolutely no reason for anything to change, until, suddenly, everything was over: Leopoldo's love had drained out, like water in an unstoppered bathtub.

The bedrooms on the first floor—Cynthia's to the right, Leopoldo's to the left, and in the middle the one for the children who had never come—opened onto the gallery. A jasmine in bloom swathed one of the columns that supported the arches. Sandals in hand, Cynthia entered her room, turned on the light, threw the window wide open to let in the scented air. In Leopoldo's room, at the other end of the gallery, the lights went off immediately, as if by agreement. Cynthia went barefoot to the parapet, tore off a sprig of jasmine, raised her eyes to the moon. Then she rushed back in, and, fully dressed, threw herself onto her frilly bed and almost burst into tears. But she didn't. Instead, she breathed deeply a couple of times, went to the bathroom, placed the jasmine sprig into a glass of water, took a shower, removed her makeup, brushed her hair—twenty-five times with the right hand and twenty-five with the left—took a sleeping pill, slipped under the covers, and turned off the light.

Through the open window, the scent of the jasmine also entered Leopoldo's room with the pale light of the moon.

Leopoldo sighed with fatigue. He was too old to indulge his erotic fantasies the way he had during his lunch break. Besides, Marisa was not his type. He hoped that, in spite of his brilliant performance, she wouldn't call on him again. Otherwise, she would force him to ditch her as quickly, if as gently, as possible. But he ran no risk: those two hours of strenuous acrobatics must have been as painful to her as they had been to him. "Good Heavens, what a bore!" Who sang that line? Maybe Don Bartolo. Unfortunately, boredom is more contagious than love. In ten years of marriage, he had been unable to infect Cynthia with his love and pull her out of her prudish, infantile terrors. And yet she loved him, poor dear; but had he, her gentle prince in a golden armor, dared graze his princess's lips with a kiss less light than the flight of a butterfly, in her eyes he would have immediately turned into an ugly toad. Indeed, his incredible conjugal adventure was only a comic parody of the famous fairy tale.

His American tamer with her invisible whip had made him jump as high as he could, as a lewd gorilla trained to obey. And, like an enslaved animal, he had ended up sharing Cynthia's revulsion with fierce voluptuousness. Bothered by the memory of how basely he had wallowed in his feeling of inferiority, Leopoldo lit a cigarette: his stifled desire had seemed to thrive on the fact that it was unrequited, and had kept growing in a soil amply fertilized with self-loathing.

This state of affairs had gone on for a few years. In that period he has filled his life with complicated love affairs. He had magnified every adventure into a passion, and had done his damnedest to be obsessed by it. He had tormented his mistresses with his jealousy, and had abandoned them, only to take them back and throw himself at their feet in self-punitive ecstasy. He had dramatized his love affairs in order to turn them into a full-time fixation that would make up for the emptiness of his marriage, and had made life unbearable to both himself and his mistresses with his valiant efforts to prolong the thought of them, if only in the shape of an annoyance, beyond the hours devoted to their meetings in the *garçonnière* in via Fillungo, officially secret but in fact known to the entire city.

Then, one day, he had realized that his escapades were no longer necessary since his desire for Cynthia had died out.

He stubbed out the cigarette and kicked off the sheets. It was over. His suffering was over and it was no longer necessary to shore it up with alternative heartaches.

On the gallery, the wicker *dormeuse*, the armchairs and the table—unnecessary props for an impossible encounter—stood out against the moonlit arches. Every year the entire set was repainted, the cushion covers washed, but nobody ever used them, not even for breakfast. Leopoldo had his served by the cook in the kitchen, at seven in the morning. Fatima brought Cynthia's tray to her bedroom later. By day, as well as by night, the gallery remained a sort of no-man's-land between two enemy trenches.

The glow issuing from the other window had long disappeared: no doubt Cynthia had taken one of her sleeping pills and was now sleeping blissfully, like a well-fed child, dreaming—Leopoldo thought—the grotesque parody of a childish dream mummified in the mind of a thirty-five-year-old woman: a cardboard Disneyland, a plush paradise filled with talking animals, but no snakes or apples.

He grabbed his robe, and shuffled noisily down to the library.

13

THE DUMBWAITER I HAVE HAD INSTALLED between the
kitchen and my bedroom announces the arrival of my breakfast
with a gentle, silvery chime. Like a reliable alarm clock, it wakes
me up at seven every morning, including Saturday and Sunday.

I go pick up the tray, and then slip back into bed and place
it on my knees. It is hard to believe that I, the son of the Rugani
widow, should now be sitting in this bed, surrounded by this
furniture, eating a breakfast that has reached me in such a
melodious fashion. A more likely prediction, for any astrologer
who might have been summoned to my cradle to map out my
future, would have involved the same scene with little Aldo,
now in his middle years, wearing a black-and-yellow-striped
jacket and preparing the same breakfast at the other end of the
same dumbwaiter.

Instead, here I am. This world—which I recognize in the
splotch of light on the corner of the rug, in the sinuous outline
of the rosewood bureau, in the particular way it resonates—is
the same one I spied on through the dislocated slat the night I
was hiding from the Germans. That timeless scene vanished
from reality without leaving a trace; its characters—a family of

rich refugees—went back to their city, whether Milan or Genoa. Some of them must have died, others must have aged beyond recognition. The villa, with its gallery, is still there—I drive by it whenever I go eat game at Moreno's—but it too has become unrecognizable: bought and sold three or four times since the war, it is now divided into various apartments, each with its clothesline, rabbit cage, and the inevitable garage with a corrugated plastic roof.

It is as if the image of that night had flashed in front of my eyes like an ectoplasm, barely long enough to show me the way to my El Dorado and cling to my mind as a constant term of comparison. Cold, cold, lukewarm, warm, hot. Burning! I got it, I am right in the middle of it. I still can't believe it.

At times I wonder, not without some dismay: will I ever get used to it? When is doubt going to give way to the belief that I am not dreaming, that I really belong to this world, and that this world belongs to me—since I not only can see and hear its inhabitants as if I were spying on them through a crack in a shutter, but am also seen and heard by them as a guest at their own table. What happens to someone who no longer has anything to strive for? What stagnant pool will reflect the vision that is now offered to my eyes—two perfectly manicured hands buttering a toast, Meissen china on the tray, the silk bedspread, the Charles X chair, the sun-streaked rug, the furniture, the curtains, the white cashmere cardigan dangling sideways like a chimp, one sleeve nonchalantly looped around the coat hanger, the other dragging on the floor? What will become of me? What is the punishment for those who have reached the aim of their lives: restlessness? boredom?

I carry the tray back to the dumbwaiter and walk to the window. In the Santini park, Violante is pulling up weeds from among her dahlias. She is wearing jeans and a blue and white striped T-shirt—a small woman in her late seventies crouching like an Arab among her flowers. She pulls out tufts of couch grass, shakes off the earth that's clinging to the roots, and then abandons them, as it were belly up, under the sun's withering rays. They are the same necessary, ritual gestures—devoid of both cruelty and compassion—with which a farmer wrings a chicken's neck.

I put my binoculars down and start getting ready, now and then strolling back to the window, while Violante, having weeded her border of dahlias, is pushing her wheelbarrow toward the toolshed. The gardener, carrying a shovel on his shoulder, meets her midway. They are almost the same age. They stop to chat a while, nod—showing, even at a distance of six hundred feet, a deep, mutual understanding—and then they part ways.

I should write all this down. But I can only write about painting, otherwise I should make it my duty to put down, in black and white—whether in the form of a novel, a play, or better yet, a musical comedy—something involving the characters of my secret theater. As it is, what will happen to them the morning when, waking up without being surprised by my surroundings—not by the silver bell, or by the Shiraz rug, or the T'ang horse—I forget to rush to the window to see what they are doing? What will become of my dear characters the day they lose their only spectator? They might have to turn off the spotlights, fold the backdrops, hang up their costumes, and then put their own bodies away in the equipment trunks.

Watching Violante from my window, I tell myself that everybody should have the right, if not to immortality, at least to a decent embalming. This is what my musical would do. It could be titled *The Taxidermist.*

Naturally, I would start with Violante, a tough customer, I'd venture, even for a real writer. So limited and yet so Olympian. And not a bit picturesque. A perfect house, a famous table, her cookbooks translated all over the world. Not to mention the garden. And the way she keeps a tight rein on everything, disregarding all that remains outside her pale. The time lapse between action and reaction must be short, the possibility of interference from outside factors must be foreseeable, if not exactly controllable. And when things don't go as planned— aphids eat her roses, her favorite son stages a tragedy and concludes it with his abrupt death—she doesn't blame anybody, doesn't tear her hair out. Instead, she cuts off the nibbled stems, buries her son, and gets back to work.

As I wash, shave, and dress, shuttling between the window and the bathroom, Leopoldo has come out of the house and driven off.

The machines in the paper mill keep on running, running, day and night, all week long, but as a rule Leopoldo does not go to the plant on Saturday and Sunday. And since his mistresses are usually married women who devote their weekends to their husbands, if he has left early, on a Saturday morning, it must be for something other than work or love. More likely— his attire confirms my assumption—he has decided to go visit his old group of friends—a history professor at the University of Pisa, a bookstore manager, a lawyer, an elementary school teacher—with whom he shares a passion for the mountains.

They are all inveterate bachelors or disillusioned husbands. They bask in an atmosphere of fervent celibacy, the sort of misogynistic and slightly bawdy harmony—barely tinged with unconscious and puritanical homosexuality—that seems to flourish in the provinces. For a period of four or five years after marrying Cynthia, Leopoldo, unable to tear himself away from her, gave up his walks in the Apuane mountains. Instead, he invited his friends home for dinner, trying to impose on them a new form of social intercourse that would also include women, thereby hoping to salvage everything, the confederacy of bachelors as well as his conjugal idyll. This state of affairs went on for a while thanks to the desperate good will of all involved, then it collapsed, a casualty of the law of gravity as well as of the oppressive boredom of those evenings.

I was invited also, with Lavinia when she was around, or with some other, temporary flame. I sacrificed myself with unremitting zeal, mindful of the rallying cry that echoed throughout the city: do your damnedest to make the American bride feel at home and avoid Leopoldo's defection.

Even Cynthia did her damnedest to make sure that everything was simple, sportsmanlike, Italian, and male. She served tortelli with meat sauce and steaks instead of her usually fanciful and exotic dinners, told the maid to take the evening off, and waited on us herself, around a checkered tablecloth.

Nevertheless, their guests inevitably fell on either side of what seemed to be a natural, and inexorable, dividing line: half of them appeared haughty, affected, worldly, the other half rustic, old-fashioned, coarse. As I could not see myself, I don't know which side I was on; but I also shared in the general dreary feeling that I was getting bored for no purpose, and that I was projecting the worst possible image of myself.

But the most grievous part of it all was that, since the dividing line passed straight through Leopoldo, in his effort to get along with everybody the poor man felt compelled to smile affectedly on one side and laugh coarsely on the other, with the result that he resembled a court jester in a bicolored costume.

Much to everybody's relief, that sorry enterprise was soon abandoned. Leopoldo's fondness for his old friends, whom he now only sees occasionally, has remained unchanged though fraught with a deep nostalgia, as if they were all dead. He still performs a certain number of rituals—the Monday morning call to discuss the soccer play-offs, the twelve bottles of wine from his own farm for Christmas—with the regularity and compunction of one who is paying a visit to his loved ones in a cemetery. As his relationship with Cynthia has steadily deteriorated, for reasons my binoculars have allowed me to guess, Leopoldo has gotten involved in a number of extramarital adventures but has never resumed his mountain excursions; nowadays, the mournful rituals that have replaced his conjugal love involve his devoting the entire weekend to his wife.

On the other hand, from my tower I have noticed that this

Saturday morning Leopoldo has left in his mountain outfit, which means that he must have revoked his sacrificial offer. I do not know the meaning of this new event, nor can I guess what its consequences will be. However, in my solitary existence as the observer of other people's lives, I have noticed that very often human relationships behave like broken, old radio sets which no rational intervention seems able to fix and which suddenly start working again after a well-placed kick—all too often and for no apparent reason, a sudden jolt manages to fix human situations that seemed absolutely beyond repair.

14

SIGMUND BURST INTO THE ROOM, followed by Margherita. She placed the breakfast tray onto Lavinia's knees, went to the window to open the curtains, and then back to the bed to switch off the light on the bed table.

"There is some young man asleep in Nicola's bed. He's naked." She announced. The total lack of inflections in her voice betrayed disapproval. "The door was open," she added.

Margherita did not like young people. She saw them as sloppy, insensitive, always ravenous, and dirty: a lot of work and no tips. "Provided there are no children," she had specified when she had started working for Lavinia. Had she liked children, she would have stayed at Fabbriche di Vallico, would have married a woodsman, and would have given birth to her own children, three or four of them. Just like her sister, who worked twelve hours a day cutting vamps for a clog factory on her kitchen table, and who, every time Margherita went to visit her driving her own car and wearing her fine clothes, looked at her without even bothering to hide her admiration, as if she were a movie star.

Only later had Margherita realized that, in fact, there was a child, a ten-year-old boy. She was tempted to quit on the spot, but she liked working for Lavinia, besides which she had learned that—for some mysterious reason—the child did not live with his mother in Milan but with his grandmother, in Tuscany.

Shortly thereafter, she had met Nicola, who had come to spend two days with his mother.

It was the long All Souls Day weekend, but the weather had been so dreadful that it felt like winter. Nicola's grandmother had accompanied him to Viareggio to catch the six-thirty-three train. He had traveled alone, like a good little man who is no burden to anybody. He had gotten out of the train, had taken a cab, and Margherita—who had gone to open the door at the first ring—had found him, standing on the doormat, holding an Alitalia bag with one hand and a bunch of anemones with the other. "I am Nicola Santini," he had said. "Is my mother up?"

Nicky had been the sweetest child and was now a dear young man. But who was the fellow sleeping in his bed?

"I closed the door," Margherita added.

Lavinia sighed. She had had an awful dream. She was carrying her old elementary-school satchel, with the drawings she had made with her crayons inside. She was wearing her white frock with the pink bow, buttoned in the back; but underneath she wore nothing and therefore had to be very careful how she moved. Sandro and a tall blond woman who looked like Anita Ekberg sat facing each other on two gilded armchairs like the ones used by archbishops in cathedrals. Lavinia had to show them her drawings, one by one, first Sandro and then the woman. Every time she turned toward him she had to make sure that Anita Ekberg could not see in between the buttons that barely closed the back of her frock, and vice versa. So, as she pulled out a drawing with one hand, with the other she immediately covered her back with her satchel. But suddenly, with a horrified shudder, she realized that she was wearing braids and that, even if she could cover the gap in her frock, she could do nothing to cover the strip of bare skin on her neck where her hair parted, and which everybody could see, unbeknownst to her, since everything that happened on that side was beyond her control.

She had woken up in a cold sweat and had rung the bell, not so much because she wanted to have breakfast, but because instinctively she felt like clinging to that sort of alarm handle hanging right within her reach. She had a terrible headache. In fact, she would have liked to sleep a few more hours, sink into darkness without a thought in her mind. In Greece it was already ten in the morning. The sun shone high on the Aegean sea. His dark, hairy, naked body—muscular belly, sinewy limbs—was lying on a brightly colored air matress. Rosylips, also naked and glistening with suntan oil, was next to him. The boat floated with a faint rustle, sails to the wind, engine turned off. Later they would swim, fish. They would stop in a deserted cove, the shore rimmed with white pebbles and rosemary bushes, to eat what the sailors had prepared. Then they would withdraw to their cabin: the sea breeze, the smell of the sea, the glare of the sun on the water would pour in through the open porthole. He was like a wolf, nervous, spare, fiery. Lavinia could see his every gesture as if she were there, with them, forced to watch and suffer.

"He is a friend of Nicola's," she said.

"How long is he staying?" Margherita inquired.

"What?"

"How long is he staying?" Margherita inquired.

"What?"

"How long is that young man going to stay? Just for my information."

"Actually, I don't know. He didn't tell me. I imagine he'll leave today. He certainly can't wait for Nicola—he won't be here for another week."

"The dog is already full of fleas," Margherita noted with a reproachful tone. One would have thought she suspected the boy sleeping in the next room of having brought the pests into the house.

A cramp twisted Lavinia's stomach. Splotches of light danced on the ceiling of the cabin. Their hushed voices uttered the sweetest obscenities. Some tea might do her good. She poured herself a cup. Better take a pill too.

"He must have gone after the sheep," she said. "Yesterday he wasn't around all day. Besides, we know he is crazy about the shepherd's bitches. . . . In any case, you didn't try to hold him back either," she added sassily.

"In any case, it is not a tragedy," Margherita retorted. "As usual, Mrs. Violante will find a way of getting rid of the fleas and will get him a collar. But I would like to know what I should prepare for lunch and for how many people."

This was definitely not what Lavinia had been looking for when she had grabbed the bell: reproaches, questions, problems. Marco, the dog, the fleas, lunch.

"Nothing, don't get anything ready. We'll have lunch at the villa."

"In that case, I'm going to lend them a hand. I can pick the vegetables in the garden." That was one thing Margherita liked to do; thank God she was in a good mood again. Lavinia swallowed another pill with a sip of tea.

The phone on the night table rang: Cynthia.

"I have decided to have a picnic around the swimming pool, is that all right? I have even invited your admirer."

"My admirer?" That word unexpectedly stirred her interest. Something in her thermostat clicked and raised the temperature a few degrees. Had Cynthia noticed something strange in Marco's behavior? Such a handsome young man, so enigmatic . . . Actually he didn't seem to be particularly interested in anybody, but if Cynthia thought . . . "Who would that be?"

"Aldo, of course!"

Aldo, of course. The best, nicest, most predictable man in the world.

"Oh, him. OK to the picnic, then," she sighed.

"Great. Get Marco on the phone. If he is still asleep wake him up. We agreed I'd call him."

Lavinia signaled Margherita to remove the tray and slipped back under the sheets, huddling around the pain in her innards.

"Please wake the young man and tell him to pick up the phone in his room."

The splotches of light quivered on the tanned, naked torso. The long, lean muscles darted with the rhythmic movement. On deck, the metallic notes of some ancient stringed instruments pelted out of the sailors' Japanese transistor like hailstones. White sea foam caressed the sides of the boat. Everything was wonderful, as usual, when she was not there: from the fathomless depths to the farthest star, the entire universe was an unperturbed sphere of pure crystal.

If only she hadn't had the silly idea of going back to the Limonaia. How could she have thought it might help? And how could she have forgotten what she was going to miss by taking leave of Violante's roof—even if she was only a few feet away, she was in a separate house, out of Violante's direct influence. Otherwise she could have run to her . . . had she been in the villa she would have done so immediately, as she was, barefoot, in her nightgown. By now Violante's outdoor tasks must have been finished: she would have found her taking care of her correspondence or working at some new cookbook.

With her hand pressed against her belly, Lavinia got up and started dressing.

15

THE BELOVED FERRARI, the European myth Cynthia had
most enthusiastically endorsed, was reserved for fast highway
driving. For shopping downtown, the old *cinquecento* was much
better. She could squeeze it in between two plane trees at the
edge of Piazza Grande, in a tiny little spot that was not marked
by any "No parking" sign and yet was always free—just for her,
one would have thought—maybe because it was a sort of no-
man's-land, a one-dimensional threshold between the street
and the square which the Italian drivers—for all their imagination, individualism, and know-how—did not seem to have noticed. It had taken someone from Columbus, Ohio to see it.

She stopped in front of the Limonaia, honked a couple of
times, opened the door on the passenger side, and waited, letting the engine idle. She was prepared to wait, sure that Marco
would be late; instead, he appeared after only a few minutes,
but dragging his feet like someone who has all the time in the
world. He smiled lightly, a perfectly harmonious creature,
without a care. He stopped to pick up a scarlet geranium and
then turned toward the car. Before climbing into it, he tucked
the flower behind his ear, among his short curls.

Downtown, Cynthia bought a few things for him: pants, T-shirts, swimming trunks, a pair of Indian sandals. They walked up and down the streets, crossing and recrossing their own paths—cigarettes, bread, shoes, groceries; up and down past medieval buildings, the Roman amphitheater, the Art Nouveau shops, the marmoreal façades; as if in a time machine shuttling over two thousand years in just a few hundred feet. Cynthia, the foreigner, knew every stone of her adoptive city and proudly showed them to Marco, while proudly displaying to the city the handsome boy who followed her quietly with a red flower in his curls.

She bought all the necessary ingredients for a hearty but simple lunch: everyone knows that twenty-year-old boys have a huge appetite and little imagination.

Leopoldo had gone before she got up, and had left word to tell her that he wouldn't be back for lunch. "Il a mis les bottes de la Garfagnana," Fatima had told her. In fact, not only were the boots missing—Cynthia had immediately checked—but so was the knapsack with its mythical vial of antisnakebite serum which Leopoldo would have never been able to use, but which he always brought along to underline the adventurous atmosphere of those excursions: no women, clean air, few words, true friends.

True friends: they were her real rivals. At the thought, Cynthia felt a pang of jealousy. Forget women. After all, what were women to Leopoldo? *Those women*—the ones he met in the *garçonnière* on via Fillungo, officially the guest quarters of the paper mill and therefore partly her property, since she was one of the major stockholders. Besides, it had even been furnished with their things, all the stuff she had discarded when she had redecorated her bedroom and the third master bedroom, known at one time as the children's room and now, quite as platonically, as the guest room. In fact, it was a room where, for as long as she had been married, nobody had ever slept, since the social life of the family was entirely absorbed and administered by

Violante. Even her own sister, when she came to visit her from the States, was a guest at Villa Grande.

She had decided to change the furniture that she had found in those two rooms because it had struck her as gloomy, indeed, quite sinister. It was probably very valuable, but so what, if it depressed her? Massive dark wood, handwoven linen, and raw silk were fine for a library, Cynthia thought, or for a man's bedroom. She knew that Violante wouldn't approve of her choice of furniture—and Lavinia even less—but she didn't let that intimidate her. She had redone the entire thing in pastel colors, laquered wood, tulle, velvet, and wall-to-wall carpeting. And when it had been necessary to furnish the apartment on via Fillungo, she herself had reminded Leopoldo of the old furniture they had locked up in a storage room. "You should use it for the guest quarters," she had suggested, pretending she believed that was indeed the purpose of the flat. Mere common sense since he would have done it somewhere else anyway, so why spend more money buying antiques when they had all that fine stuff moldering in some attic?

The last thing she bought with Marco was the whipped cream; then she loaded all the packages into the *cinquecento*, pulled it out of its niche between the two plane trees, and drove home.

Marco, prim and quiet in the passenger's seat, gazed straight ahead without talking.

"Did you like Lucca?"

"Yes."

"You don't talk much. Are you shy?"

"Shy?" To answer her, Marco turned not just his head but his entire body toward her. It was as if he had wanted to show himself to Cynthia rather than look at her.

"Or, maybe, you don't care," Cynthia went on. "Maybe you prefer to let others take care of things."

"Take care of what?"

"Of everything. Of talking, for instance."

Marco turned back without answering, the corners of his lips curled upward slightly, like two imperceptible commas that could easily be taken to suggest mild irony at a statement too stupid to deserve a reply.

"I come from Columbus, Ohio," Cynthia hastened to add. Marco gave no sign of having understood or even heard. Once Leopoldo had seemed to delight in the naive propriety of her code of behavior: gracefully keeping a conversation rolling, going to church regularly, wearing gloves even in summer. She saw herself, reflected in his eyes, just as she was, as she had been taught she should be, and as she wanted to be: clean, fresh, healthy, like an apple just picked from the tree, or a Christmas present in its foil wrap: the perfect American girl. Then, without warning, after four wonderful years, there had been a sort of click, as from a light switch, and the situation had changed: Leopoldo had started looking at her with maliciously weary eyes, and since her only other alternative was to become a pathetic imitation of something she could never be, she had preferred to hold on to herself with tenacity and devotion, the way one watches over a work of art, or defends a flag.

They drove out of the city walls and past the brief periphery.

"I come from Columbus, Ohio," Cynthia repeated in a different tone of voice, "where it is considered very important to chat amiably with the people one meets in society, as important as washing one's ears." They were driving by a vacant lot covered with all sorts of trash. A big rat crossed the street and disappeared into a ditch. "Where I live, some things are decent, others aren't. That's all." There *was* a connection, no point denying it. That relaxation of values—Lavinia's chronic lateness, Leopoldo's lazy sarcasm, Aldo's snobbishness, everybody's indifference toward religion—was directly responsible for the accumulation of trash and rats. Not to mention inflation, unemployment, bombs, cholera.

.   .   .

Lavinia was the only one missing. Aldo was in the water, leaning with folded arms on the edge of the pool; Violante, lying on an easy chair a few steps away, in the shade of the pergola, now and then raised her eyes from her book to exchange a few words with him.

And—incredibly—Leopoldo was back. In his swimming trunks, thin, dark, bent over the barbecue grill, spreading out the coal with a shovel, he smiled at his wife and the young man approaching with the grocery bags.

"I bet you bought steaks!" he shouted.

It was Marco who answered. "Right you are!"

Cynthia said, "You took all your mountain gear. I thought I wouldn't see you until tonight."

He was back, he was back! Cynthia was almost moved to tears. Now that he had given up his mountain walk with his friends, she saw it as such an innocent passion that she almost wished that he—dear love—had gone. Her heart swelled at the thought of his big boots, and that old knapsack with the antisnakebite serum which had remained untouched at the bottom of his closet for so many years.

"I changed my mind," he was telling her. "The farther I drove, the sorrier I felt to miss a Saturday with my family."

They really looked like a family, Cynthia thought: two handsome young parents with a postadolescent son, minding the barbecue surrounded by various friends and relatives.

Leopoldo was fussing with the air vent. "It's stuck . . . look at the rust. We haven't used this thing for centuries."

"You've got a big black smear across your cheek," Cynthia said. She pulled a small pack of Kleenex from her purse. "Come, let me wipe it off." She held his chin with two fingers, as one does with children, while she removed the smudge from his cheek. My husband, she thought. His receding hairline, the aquiline nose reddened by the sun, his deep-set blue eyes. The mere thought moved her: her husband.

"It is one o' clock," Violante shouted. "And, of course, Lavinia's nowhere to be seen."

Aldo started to pull himself up onto the edge of the pool, but Marco preceded him. "I'll go get her."

On his way he met Fatima, who was carrying a basket full of plates and silver. They smiled at each other. "Dans une demi-heure j'apporterai les lasagne," she announced.

16

LAVINIA ALWAYS wore soft clothes. She loathed the stiff,
rustling fabrics Cynthia seemed to favor. That woman did not
look dressed but rather packaged, like a piece of candy. Indeed,
she gave one the impression that, under the wrapping, she was
made of some edible substance. One could even guess her taste,
quite vividly: sweet, tart, a touch artificial. And the consistency
as well: Cynthia's flesh was no doubt chewy, resilient, homogeneous. Like mozzarella, or one of those brightly colored American gelatin desserts known as Jell-O.

Lavinia knotted her belt, gathering the pleats of the light
Indian cotton dress around her slim waist. Had she been able
to achieve the desired pre-Raphaelite effect, or was she only a
gangly female with a droopy face and a limp dress? One more
question: why was it that whenever she came to Lucca she
could not help competing with Cynthia, whom, after all, she
even liked, and who, in any case, totally vanished from her
thoughts the moment she was back in Milan?

The mirror did not tell her anything about the nature of her
antagonism toward Cynthia, nor in which of the numerous
layers of her consciousness it had nestled—like a small speck

inside an oyster, but one which, she knew, would never produce a pearl. Instead, the mirror reflected back the image of a gangly female with a droopy face, but decidedly pre-Raphaelite.

For a short while after Nicola's birth, she too had worn only clinging clothes—similar to those Cynthia wore, though, of course, not cut from those unbelievable American materials. Violante had accompanied her to Florence as soon as she had left the hospital and, together, they had chosen some lovely fabrics. She could still remember her bottle-green princesse: she could squeeze the entire dress in her fist. Naturally, the colors were sober—after all, Lavinia had recently lost her husband and had just given birth to a posthumous child—and the styles were simple, but so close-fitting she could hardly breathe.

Violante had been intelligent enough to refrain from objecting in the name of good taste: she had understood. Lavinia's deformed belly had disappeared; her bosom—it had been decided that she would not nurse her baby—had recovered its original dimension. "Tummy gone, tummy gone," as the character in a commercial sang happily upon waking up from a nightmare: Lavinia knew exactly how it felt. The nightmare was over; now she could forget the entire affair: everything that involved Filippo, including her horrible pregnancy.

Of course, there was a baby, but he was awfully well behaved and Violante was so eager to take care of him.

Lavinia had registered at the university, and could easily convince herself that only one short summer had elapsed between her high school graduation and her first class in Pisa—instead of those grotesque and tragic fifteen months during which she had been in turn a fiancée, a bride, a widow, and a mother.

That entire period had been erased. It was dropped, like a digamma—a letter that was once part of the Greek alphabet but had disappeared before any poet could use it. "See," the teacher used to say, "this is where the digamma was dropped and was replaced by 'rough breathing,' " a tiny mark with an unpleasant name, a negligible entity.

The fifteen months poisoned by Filippo had also been dropped, and all that was left, though rough, was merely a breath, invisible, immaterial. Her figure, outlined by her new clothes, was as slender as before. Her classmates at the university considered her one of them.

Lavinia spun around on her feet to see how the skirt swung around her legs and whether the pleats fell as they should. Was it really true that her classmates had considered her one of them? She drove to school from Lucca in her white *cinquecento* instead of taking the train; she dressed better than anyone else; she took it easy, seldom attending the lectures, and showing up for just two exams a year.

She would wait in front of the classroom door in silence, while everybody else seemed to have so much to talk about. On second thought, she realized that those had been crucial years for most students, and that, for the first time in her life, she had been at the right place at the right time rather than, as usual, arriving when the party was over; unfortunately, she had not realized it then. She had noticed that there were more people, more policemen, more posters, but she hadn't even come close to imagining that she was witnessing the passage from one era to the next. A few months earlier she had set up a boutique, she had other things on her mind. She had been shuttling back and forth between Pisa and London, buying clothes on Carnaby Street and reselling them in Italy.

Unfortunately, Biba's and Mary Quant's brilliant ideas were already known all over the world and copied everywhere: the clothes Lavinia brought back from England were identical to those one could already find in Italy, but they were more expensive and more poorly manufactured. In her first commercial venture, Lavinia had again respected the most fundamental law of her life: she had punctually arrived too late. As usual. She had started by being born late, and from that day on had always been out of phase.

As a child, in the chilly drawing room, under the mournful eyes of a maudlin Mlle. Morot, she used to leaf through her parents' photo album. The snapshots depicted elegant youths leaning against the parapets of luxury liners; her grandparents on the steps in front of their Fiesole villa; her eighteen-year-old mother in a long white skirt carrying a tennis racket, somewhere on the Isle of Wight, and then again, just a few months later, during her honeymoon on Mount Lavinia, on the island of Ceylon. . . . She adored that album, it was a real fetish for her, but looking at those photos hurt her, physically: even then she could feel a pain in the center of her body, like a burning finger marking that point as her eternal barycenter, a needle pinning a butterfly down on a sheet of white cardboard, with a Latin name underneath.

How wonderful her parents' life must have been before she was born, during those twenty long years blessed by her absence! What evil spell had transformed that young man in his cashmere sweater leaning against an elephant into that spent, worn old man who went to buy his chicken liver in person for fear the maid would pocket the change?

And this wasn't true only of her parents—everybody else seemed to have done great things in her absence! Milan had been quite a city before she got there! The friends she had made there kept telling her of a golden age, when everything was happening. Not to mention her men, whose past lives always seemed to have been far more exciting than the one they shared with her.

Lavinia listened to them with a smile that she hoped was enigmatic, or, at least, sufficient to mask the true expression on her face, the one she felt inside, as her tongue had felt the seven stitches which, invisible from the outside, had been applied to the inside of her cheek when as a child she had fallen down the stairs. Similarly, her true, pathetic face was turned inward, invisible to all, but exceedingly ridiculous to her, since she knew what it looked like: the face of someone who arrives at the party out of breath and full of hopes, only to find heaps of trampled confetti and crumpled streamers scattered dismally on the floor.

The sandals with the characteristic leather strap across the big toe were also Indian. The flat soles—of a color that would soon be matched by the tan of the foot—were to give the impression of someone walking barefoot, thus emphasizing the general suppleness of the gait and, hopefully, minimizing the fact that she was always one head taller than anyone else, with the exception of Aldo who, fortunately, was also quite a beanpole.

The poor dear, he was also quite nice, and intelligent. . . . Maybe she should have met him when he was a forger: adventurous, something of a crook. Looking at him now, no one would have believed he had had a shady past. She brought her face to the mirror and looked herself severely in the eye: "Why is it you don't like honest people?" she asked.

A voice coming from the French window brought a sybilline answer to her question: "The lasagna will be ready in half an hour."

Marco entered the room, welcomed by Sigmund. "Are you ready? Everybody's waiting for you."

He had stopped behind her; raising her eyes to meet his, Lavinia addressed him in the mirror: "Do you always sneak into ladies' bedrooms this way?"

She had given him an opening to answer her with a compliment: "It depends on the lady"; "Only when the lady is beautiful." Instead he said, "The window was wide open."

Imagine that! What was the matter with him? Naiveté? Laziness? Unfathomable wisdom? Who knew, Lavinia thought, whether he was really Nicola's friend.

"You haven't gone for a swim yet?"

"I went downtown with Cynthia. We have scarcely had time to get wet: the little Indian is already setting the table." He held out his hand to her. "Shall we go, madam?"

He seized the tips of her fingers and drew her toward the window. After crossing the threshold with her, he stopped and held her close to him as if, walking through the woods, he had silently wanted her to listen to the song of a bird. They stood still a while, gazing at the garden; then his hand rose above her elbow, stroking her arm, her shoulder, stopping at the nape, his fingers crawling through her hair.

"Your eyes are driving me crazy," he said, and at once, Lavinia was absolutely sure that he didn't even know what color they were. Maybe, she thought, he feels he has to pay me back for my hospitality.

His hand brushed against her throat, proceeded down to her breasts, and roamed randomly all over Lavinia's body, without purpose and without meaning. His face, now turned toward her, did not express any recognizable emotion. The entire scene seemed so irrelevant that it didn't even warrant her pulling back and removing that hand from her body, unless, that is, she wanted to make an insufferably virtuous statement. On the other hand, as she stood there letting him caress her, she felt she had to carry out her part of the agreement according to the habitual sequence of erotic events, and so, without even realizing it, she offered him her face and lips, acquiescently, seeing how she had already acquiesced to so much.

He did not kiss her. Instead, he said, "We picked up some steaks." With a somewhat feline fluidity of movement, he moved his hand barely enough to quite change the meaning of the scene. Now he was simply escorting a lady through a garden full of flowers, inviting her, with deference, to precede him past the two lemon pots that marked the beginning of the path.

Lavinia walked in her Indian sandals looking straight ahead. What an idiot, what an idiot. She was an idiot, but he was a scoundrel. Clearly his gesture had been deliberate, a dirty trick to embarrass her. He had left her there, leaning toward him, looking stupid and pathetic.

As she pulled off her dress in the little bamboo cabin by the edge of the pool—and immediately put it back on because she had lost all desire to display her cadaverous length and pallor in a bathing suit—she convinced herself that, in fact, Marco had not meant to offend her. He had acted on an impulse and, midway, the thought of the steaks had distracted him. In other words, he was a bastard, a two-bit egoist, whose indifference to everybody else verged on cruelty.

At the thought, she felt something new and exciting stirring inside—though maybe it had already started the previous evening but was now assuming a dimension that could be registered by her consciousness—something deplorable and viscous which, for lack of any other word, she had to call love. It was a newly born feeling, barely hatched: the yacht rocking on the quiet Aegean waters still occupied the center of her thoughts, but in the distance she could already glimpse other waters, other surfs: Marco and Cynthia—she white and soft, he slim and silvery—were playing in the pool. They really were, in flesh and blood, not as the creatures of her imagination. On second thought, Lavinia decided to undress and join them.

Fatima arrived carrying the lasagna just as Lavinia was diving in. Marco and Cynthia climbed out of the pool on the opposite side and started drying themselves with their white terry cloth towels. With a confident, American gesture, Cynthia pulled off her rose-petaled swimming cap and tossed her blond hair in the sun.

Fatima had left the tray on the table and was starting to place the steaks onto the grill; everybody was already sitting down—dry and combed in their multicolored bathrobes ("Come on, Lavinia, you're the last one as usual")—everybody except for Aldo, who waited for her and pulled out a chair so that she, hair dripping all over her lasagna, could sit down too.

17

ONE SINGLE NOTE, relentlessly whirred by the cicadas, fills the valley; the scents of the country have all surrendered to the overwhelming fragrance of cut grass; and its colors, radiating as far as the eye can see in that large circle of which the Arnolfina is the center, have all been blurred and unified by the opaque yellow characteristic of the summer sun around three in the afternoon.

I am posted at my tower window, watching the Santini park, waiting for something to happen, for the show to begin.

Of course, I am way ahead of time—what could possibly happen at this blazing hour? But I am in no hurry. The sun and the white wine drunk by the swimming pool have dilated my mental processes, which now unfold in slow motion, as if underwater, lazily spiraling along a constantly changing plane.

From up here—shuttling back and forth from one window to the next—I command an optimal view of the three houses, each of which offers me a privileged insight into its most vital center: the drawing room and, immediately below it at the base of the steps, the flower beds and borders of Villa Grande; the second-floor gallery with the three French windows—corresponding to the three main bedrooms, Cynthia's, the unborn child's, and Leopoldo's—of Villa Piccola. It is obvious that if anything significant is, or is not, to happen in those two houses, it will happen in those settings and nowhere else: anything concerning Violante, the queen, will take place in the throne room, whereas anything affecting a marriage on the rocks—whatever the reasons for its demise—will inevitably occur in the no-man's-land between the two beds.

As for the Limonaia, my princess's home, with its three huge arched windows, it offers itself to my eyes like a glass cage through whose walls I can follow not only all the gestures that Lavinia will enact as a character in my play, but also those that have nothing to do with the supreme performance, but are nonetheless meaningful to me, who loved her when she was still a gangly child in knee socks and pleated skirt, and still love her now that I am old and she is no longer young—as each new meeting fills me with adolescent languor and the yearning to offer her flowers, send her love notes with pierced hearts, and cover the walls of the city with the same peremptory words: Aldo loves Lavinia.

This morning, I watched her walk toward the swimming pool with those dragging, lazy movements of hers, as if, at every step, her hands and feet were loath to change their position, regretful of what they were leaving behind and fearful of what they were going toward, wavering between doing and not doing, deciding and postponing. The country sun had already faintly colored her cheeks; the soft halo of her hair and the rosy pattern of her light cotton dress swelled and swung in rhythm with her supple step. She seemed to be wearing an anadem of flowers, and to have been prepared by priestly hands for a cruel ceremony: Iphigenia led to her sacrifice before the departure of the Greek ships.

She was a conscious victim, indeed, quite enthusiastic, as her face bore the marks of a joyous anticipation, whose motive I immediately guessed while cursing my stupidity for having spent last night dallying in vague fears rather than getting straight to the heart of the matter.

It was the boy, of course. I had been quite lacking in the most basic mental acumen not to realize that he was exactly the right type.

Like a Leporello who has changed his master, for years I have been updating my poor Donna Elvira's love records: not out of pleasure, but because she insists on ruthlessly baring her heart to me. As a result, I know all the most essential characteristics of all the scoundrels who have mistreated her for twenty years, from the very first to the very last, starting with Filippo and ending with Sandro, the sociologist.

Of course, superficially they would seem quite different from Marco. First of all they are all grown men, and—as if stamped out by the same cookie cutter—all cultivated, elegant, somewhat snobbish, seductive, and influential. Interesting men, full of charm, as Lavinia describes them in the course of her outpourings.

She also adds, however, that with such men—top-quality, the cream of the human race—there is always a catch: they are unfaithful, sadistic, mendacious. The way she says this, one could think it tickles her pink. She manages to turn her own humiliation into some source of pride—at least when she talks to me. I sincerely, if not nobly, hope that when she is alone she doesn't find it quite as exalting. In any case, the version I hear would seem to suggest that her predilection for those wretches is a feather in her cap. She wants her men to be special; she is selective, aristocratic. She likes to aim high, and every time, she faces the consequences with a small, courageous smile.

I could strangle her when she starts singing this tune. It is as if, with utter cruelty, she wanted to build herself up at my expense. Since, needless to say, the immediate corollary to her theory is that a good man—which I have been almost by definition for over twenty years, and for which I have often been praised like an old dog, with a pat on the head and a light rub behind the ears—is inevitably devoid of charm.

And I cannot defend myself. How could I—poor, dear, loyal Aldo, always at one's disposal—say that I am also a handsome man? Cultivated, intelligent, known the world over as an art expert? A friend to artists and men of letters? The owner of a house full of treasures? Long-limbed, broad-shouldered, straight-backed, and with healthy teeth? How could I say all this without appearing ridiculous, even though it is all true?

What I can do—and never fail to—is to suggest to her that she does not love certain men in spite of the fact that they are scoundrels, but precisely because they are. Not only is this so obvious that her shrink should have told her about it long ago, but it also provides my wounded ego with an acceptable explanation for the fact that this woman doesn't seem to want to love me, as she reasonably should.

This morning, as I watched her gaze longingly at Marco, who ignored her, my theory about her vocation was quite confirmed.

That punk in tennis shoes, that pipsqueak out of nowhere, has exactly what it takes to inflame Lavinia's heart: shallow, unperturbed eyes, the inscrutable face of a second-rate idol, hair so soft and bright as to reflect the blue of the sky, sensuous lips, an air of danger—the perfect alien. Besides, he is twenty-two, wanders through the world with a knapsack on his back, and is the first to acknowledge he bears no kinship with any of us. And I am sure there are other reasons that I can't even begin to guess because of the abyss that my fifty-five years and my handmade shoes have put between us.

He has crept into our world like a virus, wagging its tail, tickling this and that organ. Now something has to happen in the organism that has so regardlessly hosted him. I'll stay posted at my window ready to detect the first symptoms of illness.

Indeed, something is happening, but not where I expected.

Leopoldo has opened his bedroom window and has stepped onto the gallery. He looks around. A few tentacles of the vines climbing around the columns have spread out toward the windows and are now creeping through the shutters of the middle room. I feel I can hear Leopoldo's thoughts as clearly as I can see his gestures. A bedroom that's been locked up for years. No children, no guests. No reason, however, to let its casements go to seed. He tears off a few stems with his hands and then goes down to the ground floor to fetch the tools necessary to finish the job.

The shutters are closed from the inside. As soon as Leopoldo has freed them from the creeper, he walks into his bedroom and, via the landing, into the middle room to thrust them wide open. From where I stand, I can see the light pour in and fill every corner. I imagine I can smell the scent—a light aroma of dried flowers—that the afternoon warmth stirs and reawakens. Leopoldo steps out onto the gallery and sits down in one of the wicker chairs.

But he is restless. After a short while he gets up, walks downstairs, comes outside. He is wearing only a pair of white trousers. Bare-chested, he directs his steps toward the Limonaia.

I may well be biased, since I am waiting for something meaningful to happen, but the way he leaves his house at this hour, in this heat, looks somewhat furtive: as if he were seeking secrecy and solitude—more than if he had snuck out in the middle of the night.

For a while, he proceeds at a fast clip, until the gravel path ends and the stone patio of the Limonaia begins.

At this point, his pace changes, and his entire mien becomes awkward and clumsy, as often happens when someone wants his actions to suggest an intention other than the one that prompted them. With phony nonchalance, he plucks a dry flower from a pot of geraniums; stops and shifts his weight from one foot to the other; takes a few steps on the patio as if he were just out for a stroll; then he turns his back to the Limonaia, picks up a rock from the ground, and throws it into the cherry laurel bushes.

Sigmund immediately shoots out of one of the windows and dives into the shrubs; after some rustling about, he reemerges, panting, with the rock in his mouth. He deposits it delicately at Leopoldo's feet, then, with a smile so wide I can see it from up here, sits still and waits.

Leopoldo tells him something in a low voice—I can barely hear a murmur—and takes a few steps toward the Limonaia. The dog picks up the rock with his teeth, places it a few inches away from the blue espadrilles, and lets out a low, discreet, but nonetheless audible yelp—sort of like a civilized little honk to remind the driver of the car ahead that the light has just turned green. Leopoldo pays him no attention and takes two more steps toward the house.

Sigmund picks up the rock again and follows him when suddenly Marco, barefoot and naked, with tousled hair and a shocking-pink towel wrapped around his loins, steps out of his room.

Crazed with joy, the dog starts running back and forth between Leopoldo's and Marco's feet, wagging not just his tail but his entire rear, arching it like a shrimp. As I watch the scene, I realize that I can only observe it, without trying to understand it; at the moment, the dog's thoughts are the only ones I can interpret. Leopoldo feels like playing, Sigmund thinks, and this is a rare opportunity. He threw the rock even though, as usual, he now refuses to pick it up and throw it again. Generally, he behaves like everybody else with the exception of Nicky. He doesn't want to hear about playing with me: "Stop it," he says. "Sigmund, enough"—everybody's favorite expression. But today it's different; even Marco has come out to have fun with us. We will all play together, a real party.

He picks up the rock and, at a gallop, brings it to the boy's feet.

I am too far away to understand Marco's words, but I am sure they are addressed to the dog and not to the man who is only standing a few feet away. He bends to pick up the rock and throws it along the path, past Leopoldo; while Sigmund takes off in pursuit, he starts walking in the same direction.

When the two men are side by side, they pause for a while and then proceed together toward the swimming pool; the older of the two confidently trampling the gravel of the path with his espadrilles, the younger one walking barefoot on the grassy edge, his hips gently swaying. Sigmund keeps running back and forth to fetch the rock they take turns throwing. Leopoldo and Marco don't seem to be exchanging a single word; now and then one of them says something to the dog.

At the pool, Leopoldo sits on the edge; Marco discards his towel, stands stark naked on the edge to test the water with his foot, and then dives in. After a few strokes, he hoists himself up on the silvery air mattress that's gently rocking with the rippled surface.

"You know, I thought Nicola was a real orphan. I mean on both parents' side," he says. Marco's voice reaches me crystal clear, carried by the sheet of water. I can't make out Leopoldo's answer but I can easily imagine it. Filippo's horrid behavior, his fall from the viaduct (Leopoldo stands up and starts walking up and down along the edge of the pool), the birth of the child, Lavinia—herself very young—who had ample reason to forget and start anew, and Violante, who had been Nicola's real mother. At the end of the speech, Leopoldo turns to gesture in the direction of the villa, and a few words manage to reach my ears. "On the other hand, Nicola has always been mature for his age. Even when he was a child, with his father dead and his mother gone most of the time, he did not seem to miss his parents. At least, on the surface. Who knows how he really felt inside, the poor child."

"I am a child too, delicate and with a fair complexion. I don't want to get burnt," Marco declares. Even from this distance, I can detect the coquetry in the tone of his voice. I can imagine his lips, halfway between a childish pout and an ironic smile. With the palms of his hands, he paddles to the edge of the pool. Leopoldo picks a jar from the small table with all the suntan lotions, kneels on the ground and starts spreading the cream on the boy's body. Now they are close to each other. They speak in a low voice and I can no longer hear them.

Sigmund has crawled into the shade of an easy chair and is now asleep.

18

'' WE COULD TRY to lift it up a bit around the temples,''
Lavinia said. Margherita, standing behind her chair, turned off
the hair dryer and unrolled the blond strand from the cylindrical brush.

"It would only last ten minutes," she answered. She placed
hair dryer and brush on the dressing table; with expert fingers,
she tousled Lavinia's hair. She pulled it up, as if to let it fill with
air, then, opening her hand, let it fall back in place. "See. We
have worked on it for half an hour, and it's already going every
which way. The only thing to do is to respect its natural inclination. The color is fine, distinctive," she said, sweetening the pill.
"And it is as soft as a child's."

Lavinia looked at herself in the mirror with dislike. Something soft and transparent (but what color was it? It had no
color!) framed her face, hanging limply, like torn spiderwebs in
chilly old attics. Respect the natural inclination—her hair's and
everything else's. Keep in mind the way things and people are:
take them or leave them. And when you take them, do not
expect the impossible—Filippo's love, Sandro's fidelity, a nice
curl in your hair—but only the best possible result. She picked

up the brush from the top of the dressing table and rearranged a strand on her forehead. Knowing what was right was no help at all.

"Thank you, Margherita," she said. "You couldn't have done a better job."

The best possible result meant that her hair was clean and fluffy; that, twenty-three years earlier, Filippo had married her and rescued her from poverty; that, today, Sandro loved her his way, that is, not at all, or almost. And what about Marco? What could she reasonably expect from him?

"If you don't need anything else, I'll go downtown with Nives," Margherita said.

Why should she expect anything from Marco? He was as innocent as an animal—a white, slightly bloodthirsty ermine, with much grace, immaculate paws, and not a doubt clouding its mind.

"Of course," she said. "You may go."

She was going to be left alone with him, provided Aldo did not drop in on them.

A touch of rouge on her cheekbones? She smoothed it on with her fingertips. Once, in London, she had walked into a beauty salon and had given the manager carte blanche. "Do what you want. See what's wrong and fix it." She had told her how much she could spend, a considerable sum. She had come to buy clothes in Carnaby Street, and midway through her purchases had reached the conclusion that the boutique was a stupid mistake. It brought her very little profit, and no longer amused her. "You must love yourself," her therapist kept telling her; it was the perfect opportunity. Her eyes had fallen onto that convincing pink-and-gold sign. She had the money. She was alone in a foreign country. All she wanted was not to have to decide anything. They had to make her over as they saw fit, without consulting her, otherwise it would all be for nothing. Someone had to give birth to her again, so that she could really emerge a different woman.

The result was disastrous. Her plucked eyebrows made her look like a rabbit, her hair color, "revamped" according to the aesthetic standards of the hairdresser, had turned into a metallic beige that made one think of car paint, while her eyes, greatly enlarged by the makeup, looked meekly bovine.

She got up from her chair, undid her belt, pulled off her bathrobe, and threw it onto the bed. Margherita was leaving through the living-room door; Lavinia saw her cross the patio, pass between two geranium pots and proceed on to the path, her straw bag strapped across her shoulder.

Lavinia slipped into a jade-colored, light cotton kimono, and opened the door that led to the hallway.

"Marco," she called.

He answered after a few seconds. "I'm here." The voice came from the living room. He was lying on the couch, a glass of orangeade nearby on the rug. He was all dressed in white: pants, espadrilles, T-shirt.

"You really look like an ermine," Lavinia said, as she sat on the low table in front of him.

"Your mother-in-law can't stomach me," Marco suddenly exclaimed. "And neither can Aldo. Those two really hate me."

"That's not true. It's all in your mind. You're wrong."

"No, I'm not wrong. I'd like to know what I have done to them." His eyes filled with tears. He turned onto his belly and sunk his face in the cushions: "I hate to be hated. I'm leaving."

"You don't know what you are saying. . . . Make some room for me." Lavinia sat on the edge of the sofa and started caressing the boy's hair. Marco remained motionless for a while, then he moved an arm slightly, and suddenly his hand was under the jade-colored kimono and between Lavinia's thighs.

Once again, as in the morning by the window, she found herself thrown off balance by the wrong gesture, which, however, having been made, could no longer be taken back and had to be brought to a conclusion as quickly and as painlessly as possible. The duet was so ridiculous as to appear obscene, Lavinia thought: her hand, tenderly and maternally caressing Marco's hair, his brisk fingers finding their way without wasting any time on foreplay. The dissonance was horrible and, once again, humiliating for her. Now she had to come to terms with the situation—as usual, clumsily and a touch too late—and get in tune with the music.

She stopped caressing Marco's hair and lay down on the couch next to him, letting the kimono slide open to reveal the pale length of her body. Just as she saw her legs stretch out and the jade-colored corner of her kimono dip into his glass of orangeade, she had the mathematical certainty that he might once more leave her in the lurch, and suddenly sit up and start chatting about this and that while she lay there, indecently spread out. As if, with Marco, she had already shared a past fraught with the disappointments and deceptions of promises made and seldom kept—just another absentminded trapeze artist who forgets to extend his arms at the right moment and lets his trusting partner fall and crash right in the middle of the ring.

Instead, this time he surprised her precisely by not surprising her: what had been begun was concluded, and his elfin body mounted Lavinia's and abandoned itself to her embrace. And she felt as if she had suddenly dilated and deepened, as if she had turned into a nest to welcome and protect something infinitely small and precious.

But later, when the little ermine snuck out of its nest and curled up in the corner of the sofa, Lavinia closed the front of her jade-colored robe and realized that there were still two hours to dinner and that she had nothing to tell that stranger, and not a clue as to how else to entertain him and fill the abyss between them.

With Sandro—whether in her apartment under the eiderdown, or at his place on the posturepedic mattress with its stainless-steel frame and black linen sheets, leaning against the pillows with their knees up and a glass of tomato juice in their hands—she fully enjoyed that magic moment of truce. For half an hour, and from both of them, words would spontaneously pour out without her having to wrest them from him or him having to yield them to her. It was a pleasant, friendly sort of chat, touching on common interests and tinged with irony, the fond intimacy of exchanging advice—don't miss that movie, read that book, the homeopathic doctor, the upholsterer, the plumber—punctuated by a "you" that suddenly echoed with an unusual brotherly timbre, the pleasure of being the same age and having a large base of common allusions on which to anchor the stories of one's personal experience.

Marco was no help to her. Silence did not bother him. Quite the contrary, one might wonder whether that nacreous look did not hide the deliberate intention of increasing his interlocutors' discomfort so as to get the better of them—he could walk without fear through the poisonous vapors that threatened her, as if he were protected by some secret antidote. She tightened the belt around her waist and, like a turtle, coiled back upon the center of her body, where the usual pain had again started to flare up. My God, she silently groaned. My God, my God. She needed someone to take care of her, comb her, pet her, cherish her, and if necessary even chide and punish her. Provided she was not abandoned in a corner, forsaken, forgotten, and forced to fend for herself. Why in the world hadn't she gone to Villa Grande as usual? It was so comforting to be in a house where everything ran like clockwork and nothing depended on her.

As comforting as men with initiative, men who came to take her out with theater tickets already in their pocket, reservations at the restaurant, and everything already clearly mapped out for the rest of the evening—political opinions, topics of conversation—including, at the end, the words and gestures necessary to bring the encounter to the right level of intimacy. Men who allowed her to listen to them with that famous enigmatic smile of hers, and just nod and drop a word here and there to show them what an attentive and intelligent listener she was, and how independent she was in her judgment since, though she always eschewed polemics, that little smile of hers made it impossible for anyone to figure out whether she agreed with what they had said or not.

She cast a powerless, forlorn glance around the room: the furniture, the rugs, the hallway beyond the door. Violante's reach stretched far, even as far as the Limonaia, where a benevolent presence could be felt in just about everything, from the soap in the bathroom and the flowers on the console table to the soft drinks in the fridge; but why, why hadn't she sought shelter, as usual, at the heart of that protective sphere?

And, above all, why had she let such a puny creature climb on top of her, that tiny little thing that now looked to her like one of those diminutive males nature occasionally enjoys producing—an impudent little toad clinging with anthropomorphous hands to the huge body of its gigantic female?

He had withdrawn into a corner of the sofa; crouched on his heels, like a fakir, he looked as if he were waiting for something to happen.

Lavinia picked up the phone and dialed 161. Six-forty. "Good Lord, I didn't know it was so late," she lied. "I must get ready for dinner."

She ran away to take refuge—alone, thank heavens—in her bedroom. Rid of Marco's presence, she could wallow in the memory of his beauty, relive, as she lay on the bed, the grace of his movements, the divine lightness of his body, the scent of his hair. She saw him abandoned in her arms, his eyes closed, while she whispered sweet nothings in his ear. Everything cohered: dream bodies have no elbows, and imaginary lovers are not always about to say the wrong thing.

Sandro and Rosylips floated on the Aegean sea, smeared with antiwrinkle lotions—heavy, awkward, and, for the time being, harmless. They spoke of expensive things, intellectual fads, exclusive places. Their drawling voices nonchalantly skimmed through the Great Issues, and fiercely churned up inanities according to the ancient model of chic humor. They got along fine.

Knew the same people. Despised the same columnist. Detested the same psychologist. Adored the same comic-strip writer. In Paris, they checked in at the same hotel. At the bottom of their respective hearts, they were absolutely convinced that there were no more than three hundred people in the world, since the tracks of their six hundred feet formed a web into which one couldn't help bumping at every step.

Lavinia smiled at the ceiling. She felt oddly indulgent toward Sandro, Rosylips, and even toward herself. Because, after all, she had also been like them, indeed, still was. She was one of the three hundred people, with their silly social games complacently delighting in all sort of trifles. And if someone made her feel like an outsider, she felt stupidly hurt for having no longer been allowed to feel stupidly complacent. She was an idiot, through and through, but it was not her fault. It was never anybody's fault, and hers least of all. She had never looked for trouble; it just happened that she had often found it, ready-made and handy. She was born in the middle of it, whether she liked it or not.

However, she now had her little ermine. Finally she had something so small she could hold it in her hand, something precious and delicate that she could never confuse with anything else she knew: it was a sliver from another world, compared to which any object belonging to this one looked coarse, opaque, heavy.

Of course, the only place where she and Marco could meet was in a dream: to be friends with him would be ridiculous, to confide in him obscene, to be tender with him preposterous; even making love with him, at least when it came to its more concrete expression, was out of balance, at least judging from the sort of disturbance that the mere thought of it stirred up in her.

She had caught an ermine: a perfect creature, wrapped, by birthright, in a royal cloak. Or was it in fact the ermine that had caught her and was leisurely preparing to tear her apart with its sharp little teeth? It was one or the other, or both at the same time. What difference could it make? She curled up around her nervous gastritis like a hen warming up its favorite chick, and fell blissfully asleep.

19

VIOLANTE STARED AT HER DIAGRAM for a long time. The lines pointed in a strange direction, and seemed to suggest an answer that she could not understand, and for which she had not formulated any question. This was the trouble with pulling things out of one's head to put them down in black and white. Out there, out of reach of whoever had thought them up, they were what they were, and had their own laws and their own destiny. No one could stop them.

The diagram had grown beyond her expectations—she had added one sheet of paper, then another—and the desk in her study was no longer large enough for it.

She had moved everything to the basement, on the old Ping-Pong table that had once been Filippo's, then Leopoldo's, then Nicola's, and was now kept down there, waiting for other grandchildren to decide to be born.

The room was enormous and silent. Nobody knew she was there. What if she suddenly became ill? She was old, very old. The certainty of death fell within an increasingly smaller span of time. By now, she could no longer die in her infancy, or in her childhood, adolescence, adulthood, or advanced maturity. She had hardly any choice left as to the time of her death; but she could still choose the place. She would have liked to die in her bed, or in the garden. Not in that cold, enormous room.

Here or there, in any case she did not have much time left. She had already buried a son—the most unnatural thing, and he her beloved son, and she not there when it happened . . . and yet she had survived. A real miracle.

The diagram had not grown by itself, of course. The fact is that when she started working on one end, she forgot the other, remote extremity, so that when she turned around the table she could no longer recognize the lines she had herself drawn.

She pulled out one more sheet of paper and tacked it onto the table.

On the top left corner she wrote: Aldo.

I saw her leave her house but until the last minute did not realize that she was coming to see me. I lost sight of her the moment she crossed the gate and was swallowed by the trees; she reappeared along the path leading to the Arnolfina, and judging from the way she tackled the slope I assumed this was not going to be just another visit.

I rushed downstairs and opened the door at the very second Violante was reaching for the small bronze bell.

Sigmund must have met her on the way. He has accompanied her here and is now confidently making himself at home. We follow him into the blue-green coolness of the living room.

It is a large, square room built on two levels. The outer level is a sort of landing which entirely surrounds the central part of the room, some thirty inches below it. This is how I found it when I bought it, maybe for reasons connected to its original function as an olive press, and I have not changed it. In fact, I have emphasized its Roman swimming pool aspect by decorating it entirely in aquatic colors. The few pieces of furniture in it—few but, I must add, of great value—seem to float; all along the walls, the paintings—my small private collection—glow and vibrate with liquid reflections.

Violante sits down in a turquoise armchair. "Did you know that last week Filippo's famous friend died?" she asks.

I knew, I read her obituary in the papers. I tell her as much.

"Well, it has had the strangest effect on me. I haven't been able to get it out of my mind. Not her, of course. I didn't even know her. Not even Filippo: not more than usually, I mean. I always think of him, night and day. What I mean is that I have been thinking of her death. I've been struck by the fact that the woman who was my son's mistress has now died—and not in an accident, but worn out by the years. Do you understand? It is as if the generation after mine had already started to die out. How can I be still around?"

"But you know why: Mafalda was much older than Filippo. Maybe she was even older than you . . . and probably sick. . . . What preposterous ideas!"

"Come, come. Don't pretend you don't understand. All I mean is that now and then things happen that remind us of the inexorable flow of time. When I heard about Mafalda's death, I felt old, that's all."

"Hard to believe, seeing you dig in your garden."

She starts laughing like a bird flapping its wings. "I know, I know. I'm doing fine. Nevertheless, I feel the need to put my affairs in order, just as if a doctor had pronounced a fatal sentence on me. I've got to do it: I have ruled like a czarina, and now they are all good-for-nothing."

"Are you thinking of the paper mill?" I venture.

"Good heavens, no! For three centuries the men of the family have taken care of it without my help . . . I have never had anything to do with it. Leopoldo is excellent, and in a few years Nicola will join him. No, I am not worried about the paper mill. I worry about what's up here." She gestures toward the window, beyond which lies the garden with the three houses and the farmland. "Walls, furniture, plants, sons, daughters-in-law, grandchildren, servants, farmhands, peasants . . . what keeps it all together. Our life."

"A kingdom," I say, with a voice full of admiration.

She looks at me askance, as if to make sure I am not teasing her. "A small one," she admits. "But it won't hold together if someone doesn't look after it once I am gone. There are things which, taken one by one, may seem mere trifles, but there are so many, so many . . . someone must go to the trouble of holding them all together. Not just keeping up with what has to be done. That too, of course, but mostly . . . I don't know how to put it. A general commitment."

"The crown," I say. "I would think a head must satisfy some requirements to be able to support a crown."

"Yes," she admits. "And the first one is to not move too abruptly. One must be unperturbable, in control. Authority is a way of walking, of speaking to the dog, of opening a door. And one can never say, 'Now I'm tired. Someone else will take care of it.' Never. To let go, even if only for a moment, is like punching a hole in a sack of corn: pretty soon there is nothing left."

"I would like to be able to tell you that I will take care of Lavinia. I'd like to, with all my heart, you know."

"I know. Loyal to the end." She smiles and strokes my hand. The armchair cushion slightly rustles under her weight. I picture her with hollow bones, covered with feathers, ready to take flight and land a little further away.

"One day," I tell her, "she'll tire of being knocked about by one scoundrel after another. Then, I'll be there, waiting for her." As I say this, my sentence appears to be utterly comic, and I blush. I assume a worldly tone and conclude, "Therefore, my queen, one of your subjects is already taken care of."

She does not want to humor me. "Did you see how they were all excited by that boy's arrival? And yet he is totally insipid. He's young, that's all. He is one of those characters who can be defined by just one adjective: young. By profession, by destiny. He won't survive his youth, he will dwindle down to two little heaps of ashes at the bottom of his tennis shoes. . . . Can you tell me what's so exciting about him?"

"I'm afraid Lavinia likes him."

"Nonsense!" Just as she's saying this, she is seized by a sudden doubt. "You think so?" But she does not wait for an answer. "You see, I've drawn a sort of diagram—I've been working on it for a week."

"Is this what you wanted to tell me about last night?"

"Yes. You are the only person who can understand me. You don't seem to lead your life carelessly. You won't be too surprised when I tell you that I like to see things clearly to be able to organize a good strategy. So, I put everything on paper."

"In a diagram?"

"Precisely." She sounds slightly petulant, as if she isn't entirely sure I am taking her seriously. "I've put everything in it, including what I don't know, like, for instance, the reason why Cynthia and Leopoldo don't get along. Lavinia says they have problems in bed. Is that possible? Personally, I don't think that what goes on in a bed is all that important." She glances at me, leaning her head on her shoulder. "This shouldn't make you think I am old-fashioned." She bats her eyelashes like an owl in the sun. "If anything I am postmodern, as Nicola says."

"It's not all that important?" I repeat.

"It depends. It may even not matter at all, believe me. One day people will realize they have given it much too much importance."

"Your diagram also includes Cynthia and Leopoldo's intimate life?"

"That is one of the unknowns. What is obvious—maybe the only obvious thing I noticed as soon as I drew the first lines—is that they need a son. In fact, all three of them do, Lavinia included. The way they have reacted to Marco's arrival has quite confirmed it. That boy's appearance has awakened something in them, some natural instinct."

"I'm afraid the instinct he has awakened in Lavinia may be natural enough but not all that maternal," I note.

Violante grabs a couple of peanuts from a Chinese bowl, pops them into her mouth, and starts pecking away at them with her front teeth while staring at me with her round eyes. "I would really like to know who has invented all these different kinds of love. Luckily, I am old enough to be allowed to speak the truth, at least among friends." She cranes her neck forward, and leans her head toward mine as if to confide a secret. "All those distinctions are phony. Love is a huge melting pot, my dear man."

She doesn't give me time to answer and goes on. "The fact that Lavinia asked to go stay at the Limonaia is in itself a sign."

"A sign? A sign of what? Besides," I continue, "Lavinia has a son, don't forget."

"She gave birth to one and I took him away from her. This is the sacred truth. It seemed the right thing to do . . . unless it was because I missed Filippo so much. I myself have never fully believed that mine was a totally altruistic gesture intended to give Lavinia a second chance. Anyway, it no longer matters. That's what happened. The fact is, now I have to give him back to his mother. I have put everything down in my diagram. Everything seemed quite simple, until yesterday: Lavinia takes her son back and, as a direct result, rises one notch on the scale of maturity, so that, when I die, she is ready to take care of everybody. Two birds with one stone, if not three or four. Order reigns, Lavinia experiences the joys of maternity, Nicola finds a young mother who will be close to him for several more years, and as for you, my dear friend, what a great opportunity. . . . Because I am sure that Lavinia would lose her perverse need to be abused. A son—even a good son like Nicola—provides a mother with all the suffering the staunchest masochist might want, believe me. She could at last appreciate the simpler joys of a happy, requited love."

"And you have drawn a diagram of all these future events?"

"Yes, my dear. And don't look at me as if I were crazy. Everybody thinks of tomorrow, of all the things they must do to carry out certain plans, and they rely on whatever data they have at their disposal. I do the same thing in a more methodical way. What's wrong with using a pencil and a sheet of paper? Do you think people who go to a palm reader are saner?"

I am so glad I figure in her projection of Lavinia's life that I wouldn't dream of criticizing her method. Instead, I ask her, "Why did everything seem so simple until yesterday?"

"I don't know. Some new things have cropped up that I can't understand. The central knot seems to have moved. . . ."

"The central knot being, if I have understood you correctly, the necessity to provoke the maturation—albeit a belated one—of Lavinia's personality. Right?"

"Yes, yes. Or rather, that's just one of the knots, the one that concerns me most. That woman must stop thinking exclusively of herself, and of the effect she has on others. Also because," she adds with a more confidential tone of voice, "one does get older, and I can assure you that after seventy to think only of oneself is not that pleasant."

I tell her that I believe her, but I stifle my deepest hope: that Lavinia will mature, like a late-bloomer, the day she notices me. That day, she will be mine: intact, the way I saw her for the first time, the sullen lip, the naked knee above the blue knee sock. In one eternal present, I will possess all the overlapping images of her I have accumulated during the thirty years I have loved her: the slender stalk gradually blooming and gradually mutating into an Oriental slave weighed down by chains; the haughty, melancholy frailty; the bright buoyancy of the hair, and the pensive eyes beneath the white veil (as she knelt by another man in the Romanesque nave); the furtive flash of a pale thigh in an eight-millimeter movie—filmed by me—of

Nicola, aged two, wrestling with his mother on the lawn in front of Villa Grande; in furs and carrying her beauty case as she boards a plane for London; in a wisteria-colored robe, with large pleated sleeves, basking in the opalescent light of her Milan apartment; in a business suit during her brief career at Olivetti.

She has never cared about anyone but herself, Violante says. In other words, she has never loved anybody: does this mean that she will only love me? That they will only love me? That entire harem of images piled up over the years to form my divine woman-in-her-forties will belong to me, exclusively?

"It seems she is always crazy about something, always pursuing some new idea. In fact, she doesn't give a damn," Violante continues. "Every time she radically redecorates her apartment . . . Remember when she developed a sudden passion for the Orient, a couple of years ago? She changed everything according to her new passion, and spent loads of money on it, but do you really think that—when the painters were gone and she squatted on her tatami mats, in the middle of all that bamboo and rice paper—do you really think she tasted even a single second of sincere aesthetic pleasure, an instant of true joy—as we could have, you with your paintings and I with my flowers? Do you really think she did?" She emits a scornful giggle and shakes her feathers. "The only thing she cared about was that crazy idea that all that stuff would somehow transform her into an ivory doll adored by the rascal on duty. That's all: she didn't care about anything else." She looks at me askance, with just one eye. "Did you go to Milan during that period?"

"Yes," I answer.

"Fortunately it didn't last. It didn't take her long to realize that she was only a barefoot beanpole sitting on the floor in a very uncomfortable apartment."

I remember. She had walked toward me with little steps, had bent her neck in a little bow, and had looked at me with a small, impenetrable smile. . . . Oh, Lavinia, Lavinia!

This afternoon never ends. The sun sits still, three quarters of the way through his journey, waiting for Violante to organize her own death. What can she offer to each of her three old children so that they will grow according to nature and, one day, die, as decently as she means to? And her offer, how can she let it lie around as if it were nothing, hoping that they will find it and pick it up on their own? But, above all, *what* can she offer them?

If it is true that they need a child to become adults, what could serve as a magical love and fertility potion for Leopoldo and Cynthia? And how to provoke that spark of recognition between Lavinia and Nicola that would allow them to readopt each other as mother and son?

She speaks of possible interventions in the warp of personal histories whose intersection she seems to occupy, and I imagine her crouching among her dahlias, busy pulling up weeds. She is so much at the center of the picture that her control over it seems unquestionable and destined to last far beyond the limits of her mortal existence.

I would really like to know how it feels to occupy such a perfectly central place in one's own world; I wonder about it with a pang of nostalgia for the man I could have been if, forty years ago, I had not torn my heart out of my body to hurl it away, as far as possible, while, from my hiding place, I watched it bounce on the floors of the stage, among the characters I had chosen as the protagonists of my life.

To be there or not to be there: it would have made a great deal of difference. What would have become of me—given my mother's ambition, my tenacity, and all the rest—had I not conceived that fatal passion, that night, behind the shutter?

I can imagine a wealthy pharmacist, with his own little villa on what once was millionaires' row—wife, two children, a false antique bed covered with a handwoven, spun-silk bedspread, a VCR, a Rotary Club card, a passion for organized tours (China, Seychelles, Las Vegas, the Arctic Circle) and slides, a vicuna overcoat: the point of intersection between what could have been and what has come true. That mythical piece of clothing serves me as a metaphorical bridge between the two existences. Without regrets, I leave the pharmacist in his little world and turn toward the image of myself as I really am, as I have chosen to be, solitary and eccentric on top of a tower, behind binoculars.

20

IF I ONLY KNEW WHAT'S on his mind, Lavinia thought. There was no exception: all men shared the same inhuman habit of leaving things hanging. Was it so unreasonable to expect that a carnal encounter be granted if only the slightest meaning by a few words? She felt herself blush: the warm wave that was invading her flowed down her arms all the way to her hands, changing their color. Obviously, she couldn't ask for anything. She would rather cut out her tongue.

This was the problem: what one needed the most was, generally, precisely what one should never ask for. Never ask for an explanation, never give one, never write letters, never demand anything, never complain. Nobody knew those rules better than she; just as nobody transgressed them with as much stupid obstinacy. To know certain things did not help. One also had to discover the right formula to act according to common sense: it would be a new Columbus's egg, and it would radically change her life.

She got up and, daydreaming, started preparing for dinner. It was sure to be the simplest trick, a brilliant little gadget, like a zipper. She could get rich selling the patent: she would rid the world of all its heartaches. Because it was just a habit, an addiction, like smoking: dangerous for the person addicted, and annoying to others. She would be able to love Aldo; but then again—and suddenly she felt as if she were hanging in midair, as if the ground had caved in right under her feet—he would be able to stop loving her. Could such an unnatural thing happen? Could he stop loving her or, even worse, fall in love with someone else? She pictured him sitting at the head of the table in the Arnolfina dining room, surrounded by friends, and, sitting directly opposite him at the other end of the table, an attractive woman, his wife. She might even be young, younger than herself. After all, he was a handsome man, and famous at that, a real authority in his field. . . . The attractive young woman kept her eyes fixed on the other end of the table, gleaming with the certainty of a secret understanding. Hey you, down there, beyond all those people, do you remember? Do you know what's on my mind? And he would answer with a similar look. It was an intolerable thought. She shooed it away and concentrated on her appearance.

She opened her wardrobe and pulled out one dress after another. Her mind turned back to Marco. The question was: what to do with that twenty-year gap? When a boy is attracted by an older woman, what seduces him most, the fact that she is older or the fact that she looks younger? What would be the point of showing up in a ponytail, jeans, a pink T-shirt, and espadrilles if in fact he liked the idea of being involved with a lady?

Marco knocked on the door. He was squeaky clean and had a sweater tied around his neck. He looked like a young boy on his first date.

"I'm going ahead, I have to stop at Cynthia's," he said.

"Fine, go ahead."

Through the window, Lavinia watched him walk away. She couldn't dress like a young girl, it would be grotesque.

Until a minute ago she had been trying to decide what was the best thing to wear; now, having piled up all her dresses on the bed, she was looking around disconsolately trying to figure out which one was the least bad. Maybe a St. Laurent and high heels. But in high heels she was over six feet tall, a real camel.

21

I HAVE COME BY to pick her up at eight-thirty. I wait for her to be ready and escort her to Villa Grande. The jets of the automatic sprinklers fill the air with a slight buzz, the nightingales sing, the flowers exude their fragrances, the first star twinkles in the still-light sky: everything in Violante's garden is behaving as well as could be wished. As we cross the jasmine bower, I slow down, and take Lavinia's hand between mine.

"Wait a second," I sigh. "Let me look at you. You are so beautiful I can't find the right words to tell you."

"Really? You think so?" she answers nervously, patting the hair on her forehead. "If I could only tame this hair." Then she adds, "I wish I were dead." She holds her words back for a minute, and then lets them all pour out on top of me: Marco's hand on her breast as they were walking toward the swimming pool, their lovemaking on the couch, their silence—unbearable to her, while to him . . . "Have you noticed it? He looks so indifferent, so irresponsible: the entire burden falls on us. To speak or not to speak, to take an initiative or not to take it. As if we had conjured him up from nothing, as if he were a dream of ours, a child of our fancy, and it were up to us to set him in motion. . . . Are they all like that at his age? Do you think Nicola is like him?"

"Nicola . . . ," I begin. I would like to keep the conversation on the subject of her son, to keep it away from what I suspected and now know, and will have to hear from her lips down to the last word. But she does not allow it. She interrupts me and goes on. "He doesn't even try to understand or to be understood, he moves among us in a condition of total incommunicability, and doesn't seem to be a bit bothered by it."

"To tell you the truth, it doesn't bother me either. He has come, he will go, we'll never see him again: who cares whether we have had a human relationship? I don't, and neither does he."

A few minutes have been enough to demolish the entire scene. I hate the nightingales, the sprinklers, the flowers, the stars. I only wish I could go back to my tower and didn't have to see anyone except through my binoculars.

Fortunately Violante seems to want to get through the evening as quickly as possible.

"We are all tired," she says when she sees us approach the loggia of Villa Grande. "We'll all go to bed early."

She is lying on an easy chair, smoking a cigarette. Cynthia and Leopoldo are sitting next to each other on the bamboo couch, with Marco curled up on an emerald cushion at their feet. The boy's head is leaning against Cynthia's knees and her fingers play with his hair. Her diamond ring and polished nails sparkle at every movement. Leopoldo is saying, " . . . quite possible that tonight you will have a fever and that tomorrow you'll be peeling all over."

"Right now I am just very hot," Marco answers.

Lavinia pauses briefly under the arcade, then takes a few faltering steps toward the group of chairs. She looks around anxiously, as if to choose to sit in one place rather than another were a vital question that left absolutely no margin for error. I realize how much she wishes she were the sort of woman she

is not: casual, self-confident, capable of making the right movements to achieve the desired ends, which in this case could be
to take three long strides toward the bunch of cushions on the
corner sofa, grab one, toss it on the floor next to Marco, and
then let herself gracefully drop onto it, at the center of that odd
little family, throwing it off balance and reclaiming what was
hers.

Instead, she comes back to me, grabs my arm, and, peremp-
torily rubbing her breast against my elbow, tows me along
toward a small sofa with two seats. For the entire evening—
which fortunately lasts only a short while—while Marco lets
Cynthia and Leopoldo baby him, she flirts with me with a dark
vengeance.

She is still clinging to me as we leave to go back home.
Cynthia and Leopoldo are walking ahead of us with Marco in
the middle, all three clasping each other, partly because of the
wine they have drunk, partly because of the narrowness of the
path, and partly to support the boy, who seems to be getting
a bit feverish because of all the sun he was exposed to in the
afternoon.

At the fork with the path leading to Villa Piccola, they whisk
him away with a perfect sleight of hand. "I have an American
lotion for your shoulders," Cynthia says. "Come have a glass
of orange juice with us," Leopoldo echoes her. Then, almost in
unison, turning back toward Lavinia: "We're going to put him
to bed in the children's room," they say with laughing voices,
as if playing a very exciting game.

All three disappear in the darkness, pushing and pulling one
another, shouting and answering the nightingale's song
through the warm summer night. Then, as we walk on past the
fork leading to the swimming pool, they reappear through the
arches of the gallery—the windows all wide open, the lights all
on—unfolding sheets, billowing them out in midair, as in a
scene out of a play.

22

I SUSPECTED IT from the start and am every day surer of it: this is a special summer. Time hiccups on: now it flies, now it drags on as if to sum itself up. This afternoon Violante's strong little hand has pulled in the reins a bit so as to allow both her and me to catch up with what has been going on and look around ourselves, impartially, as if people and things were sitting around us like the knights of the Round Table: without hierarchy, without before and after, just one next to the other, offering themselves to a benign general view. Thus both of us have contemplated our respective landscapes, and pinpointed where our two horizons overlap and our programs—my dreams and Violante's strategies—could usefully join forces.

But now everything seems to move faster than usual—first the quick dinner, then the telephone ringing the very minute we stepped into the living room of the Limonaia, and Lavinia letting herself collapse on the sofa with a long moan: her son, from New York.

Lavinia has picked up the phone, and is now holding the receiver glued to her ear; and yet, Nicola's distant voice resounds through the room as if it had passed through her body and, amplified by it, had reached my ears loud and clear. He should have spent one more week in New York, he says, but he has changed his mind. He is taking advantage of a special nonstop flight to Pisa. He is calling from the airport just before boarding. In a few hours he will land at San Giusto.

Even this phone call seems a trick of time: at once absurd and yet exceedingly significant: first of all the conversation between today and tomorrow—ten past six in the evening in New York, and ten past midnight here—and secondly because Lavinia will barely have the time to take a nap before jumping in her car to go fetch her son at the Pisa airport at seven tomorrow morning.

It is as if the three of us had found ourselves at the point of intersection between past and future. As I am making a mental note of this, I suddenly realize that this is precisely the peculiarity of the hours I have lived since receiving Violante's note inviting me to dinner: we are all teetering on the edge of time, in a continuous present which my old friend could easily represent in her diagram as the very point where the two circles of the infinity symbol touch.

When Lavinia hangs up, Sigmund bursts into the living room like a shot and cheerfully leaps onto his mistress's lap. Hugging him to her breast, she stammers, "N . . . Nicky's coming home," and bursts into tears.

I hope that those tears, in unconscious submission to Violante's projects, represent a sort of liquid bridge between the anguish of the lady brutally neglected by both her old and new lovers and the feelings of the mother moved by her son's sudden return; and maybe also—in a few minor drops at the corner of the eyes—a token of gratitude, however absentminded, for the presence of two faithful creatures, one fuzzy and wriggling in her arms, and the other dressed in white linen, standing stiffly by an armchair.

23

LEOPOLDO HELPED HER make the bed, his fine dark hand smoothing down the sheet with long strokes that ran parallel to those made by her white chubby one. "You sit still," they had told Marco. "You have a temperature, and besides, three people cannot do this." They had lent him pajamas—the right size. The two men, Cynthia thought fondly, had very similar bodies, the same form filled with different substances: muscles and bones in Leopoldo's case, and some mysterious substance, as delicate as the flesh of a fruit, in Marco's. It moved her perhaps, she reflected, because she was a little tipsy. All three of them were.

She went to the bathroom to fetch her American sunburn lotion; she glanced at herself in the mirror and saw herself as very blond, very rosy, with no hard lines or edges: curves, planes, and colors gently shaded into one another culminating in the harmonious brightness of her hair. She smiled at her reflection and her eyes filled with tears. She felt that familiar delight—like an infinite sweetness painfully pressing to be released. Nothing new to her. Other things had provoked it in the past: her mother approaching her bed, centuries ago, to give her something, something that could have been either medicine, or a scolding, or a present; the pages of certain books which she mentally recited to reproduce the same agonizing fullness of the heart: "The candle, by the light of which she had been reading that book filled with anxieties, deceptions, grief, and evil" (Anna Karenina's death was her favorite passage), "flared up with a brighter light than before, lit up for her all that had before been dark, flickered, began to grow dim, and went out for ever." No, it was not a new emotion, she recognized its quality; but she had never, ever felt it to such an extent. This time it was infinitely larger, it filled her up and kept on growing, giving no sign it might be about to stop.

Marco—hair tousled, eyes shining, and face flushed above Leopoldo's blue pajamas—was already in bed.

"Are you thirsty? Leopoldo could go downstairs and get you some fresh grapefruit juice. Would you like some?"

"Yes, please."

Leopoldo tiptoed out of the room. "Poor baby, so sick," Cynthia murmured. She was panting slightly, as if she had run upstairs. She sat down on the bed, placed her hand on Marco's forehead. "Poor baby, poor baby." She moved toward the bedstead and leaned against the pillows. "Show me your back." She helped him remove the pajama top and made him lean over across her lap. He was as light as a child and much more docile. She gently rubbed his back with her American lotion, while through the fuchsia-colored silk of her dress she felt his breath damp and warm between her thighs.

That was the last sensation of the night Cynthia could remember with any precision: time—twelve-thirty; place—the children's room; cause—the breath of a feverish boy through a silk fabric; characters—she and Marco.

Up to that moment she could still clearly distinguish the boundaries between all the things that had really happened and those, however happily similar, she had wished would happen. But later everything got all tangled up: other things happened, unless she had dreamed them or dreamed of dreaming them. Had she really drawn that child to her bosom, and had he really placed his trusting hand on her white breast as he suckled it with closed eyes? And when had Leopoldo come back, how had he come into the game, what role had he played, and ultimately, when had he picked her up in his arms, carried her down the gallery, laid her down among the virginal ruffles of her bed, and loved her, quietly, not to wake up the boy sleeping in the next room?

The next morning her husband was still by her side. The shutters had been left open, and the daylight pouring in through the jasmine-trimmed arches lapped the lace of the rumpled bed with its green ripples. Leopoldo felt Cynthia move and, without opening his eyes, stretched his arms toward her and clasped her against his body—a gesture he had never had the opportunity to make, but must have dreamed of over and over again for years, Cynthia thought with a shudder of happiness, because it felt so familiar, as if it had happened every morning since the day they got married.

"Hi there, blondie," he said to her. "We'd better get a larger bed, soon." He changed his position and let out a groan. "I'm aching all over."

"We'll ask your mother," Cynthia answered. No use buying a new bed with all the things they had at Villa Grande, she thought. Mentally, she moved a few pieces of furniture from one house to the other until she had reached a satisfactory balance from an aesthetic, economic, and emotional point of view.

As she was refurnishing the children's room, her imagination stumbled against an obstacle, an object out of place, Marco's sleeping body. They had to transfer him back to Lavinia's as soon as possible.

She tried to remember. Or was it better to try to forget? In fact, she decided, it did not matter: the things that had happened that night in the room next door—granting that they had happened—fell so far beyond the bounds of any law that they would automatically slip away from a reality with which they had no connection. In any case, Nicola was about to arrive; his presence would put everything back into place. Cynthia loved and trusted her nephew. There was something strong and authentic in him. Paradoxically, he reminded her of her grandfather, from Jacksonville, Texas, who read her the Bible every night—odd that it should be Nicola, the baby of the family.

Only for the time being, she thought, and cuddled up in Leopoldo's arms, pressing against him. They would have a boy right away—at thirty-five, she had no time to waste—then a girl.

"A boy for you and a girl for me," she sang mentally. "Can't you see how happy we will be?"

24

LAVINIA TURNED ON the headlights and, murmuring a prayer, drove into the darkness of the San Giuliano tunnel. She was a good driver, but had to overcome a great many fears: vertigoes on viaducts, panic at the mere approach of a truck, claustrophobia in tunnels. The prayer poured out of her mechanically, in spite of herself—a relic of the past. She had been brought up by parents so old they could have been her grandparents; as a result, the education she had received was far more old-fashioned than that of her schoolmates. The same fate had befallen Nicola, brought up by Violante, his actual grandmother. He had also gone through a religious discipline—like any other discipline, it did not require or propose any conviction; it had only been a formal obligation, like a polio shot. It was part of the system of norms—such as good manners, personal hygiene—that governed his life: to stand up when a lady entered a room, to brush one's teeth after each meal, to tidy up after playing, to speak only if addressed when sitting at table, to say one's prayers before going to sleep.

He took everything so seriously. Like that evening . . . how old was he? Four, maybe. It was during the tenure of Mademoiselle Claudine, the French governess. Kneeling by the bed, in his yellow pajamas, dead tired after a day of romping in the fields with his dog, he was drooping with sleep, unable to keep his eyes open.

"Allons-y, Nicky, dis vite tes prières," Mademoiselle was telling him. Lavinia was already dressed, ready to go out. She had stopped by the door so as not to interfere with the ritual established by the governess.

"Commence: Père Eternel . . . ," Mademoiselle urged him.

"Père Eternel," Nicola said.

"Et après? Vas-y, Nicky."

"Père Eternel . . . Père Eternel, sur un arbre perché, tenait dans son bec un fromage."

Mademoiselle, who had little or no sense of humor, was honestly shocked. "Mais voyons, Nicholas! Fais donc attention!" How could he confuse the Paternoster with one of La Fontaine's fables?

Nicola, now quite awake, his little face dismayed and his chin all puckered up, really looked as if he considered himself guilty of some impiety. So, Lavinia had entered the room and had picked him up—a warm, moist little bundle. She had held him tight and had whispered, in his ear so that Mademoiselle would not hear her, "Don't worry, my love, I'm sure the Good Lord had a laugh!"

Oh, if she could always find the right words! If she could only feel as close to someone as she had to her child that evening!

She went on rehearsing the same scene in her mind—his yellow pajamas, his naked feet crossed at the toes, pink soles turned upward, his serious face. . . . "Père Eternel, sur un arbre perché . . ." She lingered over the details, delighting in the feelings they stirred up in her, while she drove down the wind- ing road, under the plane trees of the boulevard, across the Arno, and looked for a spot in the parking lot. "Don't worry, my love, my baby." If she could only have him back at that age, and even earlier, when he was born, and start everything anew, from the beginning. . . . Suddenly, through the buzz of the crowd waiting at the airport, she heard a voice right behind her say, "Mother."

He drove the way back. She curled up in the passenger's seat so that she could see him more comfortably. He looked much more like her than like Filippo; she had never noticed it before.

"You have grown," she told him. Too late, too late. How could she pick up a six-foot-four man in her arms, wipe his tears, tuck him in bed? She told him how she had decided to reopen the Limonaia, but forgot to tell him about Marco. He was the one who asked. "Has a friend of mine come by?"

So it was true, after all, he had invited him. A good fellow, a land surveyor at Sesto San Giovanni. "Awfully shy. I wonder how he managed to face all of you without my protection." Every year, on the occasion of his village's patron saint's day, he went back south to visit his family. "He wrote to me in April to ask me if he could stop by on his way down, and I told him to come. I didn't know I would come back later."

A good fellow, a land surveyor at Sesto San Giovanni. And she had mistaken him for a bloodthirsty little beast, an ermine!

Once in the driveway, Nicola honked according to a special code that told his grandmother and everybody else that he had arrived. "Let's head straight for the Limonaia," Lavinia said. "Home."

25

GET HOLD OF TIME, and gather all its moments together so that they won't disperse like a flock without a shepherd. Each instant should mark at once the accomplishment of an old commitment and the promise of a new one. Never live "at random," never say "I can't." Above all, and most crucially, never look for an excuse: to reign simply means there is no one to call in sick to.

Violante put her pencil down and drew a small circle around the main point of intersection. That was undoubtedly the navel of the entire plan. All the lines had almost spontaneously converged there, aligning themselves with utter clarity.

And yet, somewhere there must have been a mistake because every time she tried to insert the last and most important datum into the diagram, everything fell into disarray and the drawing became a shabby, casual tangle meaning nothing.

Everything had worked according to plan until the very last. When Nicola had called her from the New York airport at midnight, she had given him the phone number at the Limonaia: "Call your mother and arrange everything with her." As she had expected—and much to her dismay, but it couldn't be helped—there was an immediate change in the tone of the distant voice. An imperceptible variation had crossed the ocean and reached her ears: a controlled tremor, happy incredulity, impatience. "Why, are we staying there this year?" "Yes, the two of you, you and your mother."

She heard steps coming down the stairs that led to the basement.

"Nives? I am here."

The steps stopped a moment, and then resumed, more rapidly. Nives appeared through the doorway.

"I've been looking for you everywhere," she said.

"What's the matter?"

"Nothing. But you are always disappearing."

She's also beginning to realize that I am old, Violante thought. She's afraid I might fall sick and die alone in one of these deserted dens. She looked around the enormous room, quite empty but for the Ping-Pong table. "It's freezing down here."

"It's because we are underground," Nives said. "Besides, this room is so huge."

"I know. The entire apartment where I was born, in Parma, could fit in it. Twice. For a whole year, after I got married, I kept getting lost in this house."

"Me too, at first. I cried for days on end, remember?"

"I certainly do. But then we both managed fairly well, don't you think?"

"I'd say so."

Violante dropped her pencil into the silver cup, among the others. "What will my daughter-in-law do when I am dead? And please, don't tell me, as you usually do, 'Madam, don't even think of it.' You think of it, too. That's why you're always watching me so closely. You don't want me to die in the wrong place."

Nives hesitated. There were so many little things Violante had been forgetting in the last few months: instructions to give, bills to pay. And Cynthia had punctually, and quietly, done it for her, without her noticing it. Should Nives tell her? Would she feel reassured or humiliated by the certainty that everything could go on even without her? Ironically enough, when Violante said "my daughter-in-law," she generally referred to Lavinia. Just imagine . . .

"Your daughter-in-law will do very well," Nives said.

"You think so?"

"Don't you worry. She has already learned a great deal. You needn't worry about a thing, I assure you."

They heard a brief honk in the distance, then another, and then a third: Nicola's signal.

"He's here!" the two women said in unison.

26

I DON'T KNOW whether it has all happened because of Violante's diagram, but I'm tempted to believe so. I have often been convinced that thoughts, once down in writing, tend to evolve rapidly toward reality. This is how it was with the Master of the *Virgin in Red,* who started existing after I wrote about him; I hope the same thing will happen to my kingfisher.

But, to get back to the diagram, even in this case one could say that things—which had long been ready to happen—were waiting to be methodically drawn on paper to become true. As the events of this Sunday keep unfolding, I seem to hear each of them produce the sort of click that occurs when a gear locks into place, setting the whole machinery in motion.

First of all there is the omelette that Lavinia prepared for Nicola in the kitchen at the Limonaia: there is nothing sensational about this scene, indeed it may not even be the first meal Lavinia has prepared for her son. And yet, it is as if, in every gesture she makes as she bustles about the kitchen, and in the way he sits waiting at the table, there is a new intensity of meaning reminiscent of the last scene in so many nineteenth-century novels—"Yes, my lord, I can no longer conceal the truth: I am your mother!" "You . . . madam . . . my mother!"

Drawn by the sound of the horn, we all gathered in front of the Limonaia: first Violante and Nives, followed by me, and then Leopoldo and Cynthia, hugging and visibly happy. A definite click. In the course of the night, I saw enough of what was happening beyond the windows of Villa Piccola to be quite confident that even there they have found the right gear. The last to arrive was Marco, with a red nose and the circumspect movements of someone with sunburnt shoulders.

"I'm sorry I wasn't here when you arrived," Nicola apologized kindly. "Can you stay a little longer?"

"I'm afraid I can't. My folks are expecting me tomorrow."

"I'm sorry," Nicola repeated. He glances at his watch. "For me it is four in the morning," he explains. "I really need to take a nap."

We all gather around him while he eats his omelette; Lavinia hovers attentively. Then we let him go to sleep and withdraw to the pool for a quick dip.

The day is very hot, but we can hear thunder in the distance.

As we are walking down the path I hear another click: I have found a solution to the main problem in Violante's diagram, a perfect solution, just as I have located the exact place where Violante's plans seemed to go wrong and where the mechanism she had set in motion has clicked by itself, automatically correcting, as the most sophisticated machines often do, the human error.

Cynthia grabs my arm and pulls me aside.

"Just a second," she tells me. She asks me for my pen and writes a telephone number on a matchbook. "I'm counting on you," she whispers. Leopoldo, Lavinia, and Marco are walking a few steps ahead of us; Violante and Nives have already turned toward Villa Grande. "It's about the Ferragosto procession," Cynthia goes on.

"The procession?"

"Yes, the procession that goes through the park."

"I know. What about it?"

"We are leaving, my husband and I. We want to take a trip somewhere, the two of us, alone. We are leaving tomorrow."

"I'm delighted to hear it."

"I won't be here for the procession. This is what I wanted to tell you. It's about the flower carpet. I suppose you know that once the tenant farmers used to go to the olive groves to gather the wild thyme they then offered to their masters to make the green background for the flower carpet."

"I know. They still do it. That's what I like best: that fragrance, midway between incense and myrtle, Christianity and paganism. Last year I invited some Japanese friends. They were so excited, they must have taken a thousand pictures!"

"But things have changed a bit. The tenant farmers haven't gone to gather wild thyme in the olive groves for the last four years. Time, my dear, has acquired a value it did not have in the past. Why, it's already hard enough to convince them to go gather the olives!"

"But I remember the fragrance was there last year, as it has always been."

"I've been taking care of it myself. I secretly order the wild thyme from Bruschini, the man who sells funeral garlands." She hands me the matchbook. "This is his number. Remember, you must call him four or five days ahead of time. And make sure that Violante doesn't know. No one does, except for Nives. She knows. We have been doing lots of things in secret, she and I. Violante is no longer a girl, poor dear."

Click. The new queen is ready to take Violante's place when the moment comes. But it is not Lavinia: and this is where Violante's plans have gone wrong, where the curves she has drawn have taken a different direction, refusing to follow the one traced by her pencil.

How could she possibly think her place would be filled by Lavinia! Not only is she not the right woman, but the days of natural succession are long gone. Today, it takes a good-willed

barbarian, a parvenu in love, to devotedly pick up the spoils—
someone like Cynthia, coming from far away, like an explorer
full of enthusiasm and respect for the exotic places she is going
to discover, strong and disciplined. Like me, in a way: I too
come from afar and don't give up easily. Or like Violante herself, the daughter of a poor musician from Parma. But not
Lavinia. Nives has certainly known this for sometime, and
without the help of diagrams. As Cynthia just said, "We have
been doing lots of things in secret, she and I."

27

MARCO HAS REGAINED THE POWER of speech and lost all his glamor. He is no worse than many others. A bit pretentious—like someone who tries to impress by using supposedly elegant words. The poor thing is trying to dazzle us with his rather boring knowledge of all the brand names of sportsclothes, shoes, cars, whisky, boats. "Even at the level of pure economic calculation," he says, "the optimal selection is always the one involving the authentic product."

It is more than obvious that nobody—not Lavinia, nor Leopoldo or Cynthia—cares to listen to him. They had thought he was a special creature from a different world: beautiful, mysterious, and slightly pernicious. How can they possibly forgive him for being just another young man begging to be liked who says, "By now even the general public has been sensitized to Timberland"?

There is absolutely no doubt, judging from the polite way the conversation is proceeding, that they are all counting the minutes to Marco's departure. I couldn't even say whether he is aware of how vain his efforts are to appear cool and worldly:

I truly hope he isn't, because all my jealousy of him has vanished to be replaced by incommensurable pity.

They are speaking among themselves—Lavinia, Leopoldo, and Cynthia—occasionally glancing at Marco with vacant eyes that do not seem to recognize him. Now and then, they slide into the water, lean with an elbow on the edge of the pool, and let their legs float behind them.

Lavinia looks longer and whiter than usual. Her drawling, slightly querulous voice grates on my nerves unbearably.

For the first time in my life I try to imagine—not without some regret—what my life would have been like if, on that memorable night when everything started, instead of being seduced by the vision of the table setting, the ancient domestic, and the old woman in her fur stole, I had been inspired with a simple but natural feeling of rebellion. Indeed, this is a very plausible third hypothesis, besides becoming the man I am or the pharmacist with a passion for organized tours—which, however, I have never seriously considered. And yet, it could have happened. I could have devoted my life to fighting that world instead of struggling to be part of it. I could have fought to make sure that no one would ever have to endure a crooked kitchen or a cracked cup with a greenish rim. It would have been enough to replace one detail with another, equally plausible, one. At this very moment, I find Lavinia so detestable that I enjoy imagining a slightly different starting point. Let's assume, for instance, that thirteen-year-old Aldo Rugani had a poorly developed aesthetic sense and a strong bent for moral outrage. It would have been enough to change everything. He would have been appalled by the meaningless waste of all that luxury, by the inanity of the conversation, and the imbecility of all that formality. I turn my eyes to Lavinia, squatting on a cushion, wholly absorbed in a profound study of her left knee, and shudder at the mere thought of her affected pronunciation, at her utter uselessness.

Not to mention myself: the deft forger who has always thought of himself as his most successful forgery. What am I, in this case? The fake of a fake?

"You said you're leaving this evening?" I ask Marco.

"I have to, yes."

"If you come with me, I'll take you to Poveromo to have lunch at a friend's, and then I'll drop you off at the train station in Viareggio. You'll meet two very interesting people, you'll see. He—he's more than a friend, he's my mentor—is not only the greatest living art critic, but also one of the nicest, least pretentious people I know."

"But then I won't see Nicola."

"Who knows how long he's going to be sleeping," Lavinia immediately interposes. "You'd better take advantage of Aldo's offer."

I stand up. "Come on, let's go. What are we waiting for?"

As I am drying myself, Lavinia comes out of the pool and approaches me. "When are you coming back?" she asks.

"No idea. It depends."

"Will you be back for dinner?"

"I don't know."

She pulls a long face, and looks at me with eyes that are at once pleading and resentful. I know, at the bottom of my heart, that soon my usual feelings for her will again take over, but for the time being I identify with Sandro, the sociologist, or one of his predecessors. For a moment, I enjoy being the very character I have hated and envied for years: the sort of man on whom Lavinia has lavished her demanding and sticky attentions.

I tell myself I am crazy and that I am going to be sorry, but I am acting to get out of there without answering her plaintive questions with a promise.

"What do you mean you don't know!"

I find an excuse—as I increasingly feel like Sandro, the sociologist—a half excuse since there really are some photos I want to show to Levi, but that wouldn't take more than an hour and

I could easily be back for dinner. "I must talk to Levi about the painter I am working on. I don't know how long it will take. I may even spend the night."

After all, I think, I could really spend the night at Poveromo. I have lots of things I want to tell Levi. I want to talk to him about my lansquenet painter before I send the book to a publisher. The mere thought of the work I have ahead of me suddenly fills me with excitement. I run away dragging Marco along, and on the way I keep thinking of the little kingfisher perched on a tuft of bullrushes.

28

I SPENT THE ENTIRE DAY at Poveromo. We sent Marco off swimming with my old friends' grandchildren, and I stayed home with them to talk about Martin Lansquenet. Their home is quite far from the beach, has two trees full of apricots, a small pergola, and a vegetable garden in back. Elvira, Levi's wife, having worked in a bank for forty years, retired six months ago. Now that she has the time she has started raising chickens. While David was examining the photos I had brought him on the cast-iron table under the pergola, Elvira showed me the chicken coop the two of them had built together with some wire fencing and varnished wood. Chicken and guinea hens were roaming freely all over the place.

"I lock them up at night because of the foxes," Elvira said. "They're much better when they are allowed to scratch about. They eat earthworms, grass. They've even eaten all my flowers." With a lash of her apron, she shooed a fat white hen away from a geranium stump. "When is your kingfisher going to be ready?"

"The book should come out in the fall. I'm just about done."

"It must be nice to have a book published. You're lucky, the two of you," she said waving her apron in her husband's direction.

"Why, you're not?"

"Yes, I'm lucky too. We have left our house in Florence. Now we live here year-round. I have my chickens, my garden. And I have him. And in the summer we have our grandchildren. What more can I want? When some of his stuff gets published I am as excited as he is."

I am sure she has listed the reasons for her happiness in the exact same order they occupy in her heart; I find it very wise.

We waited for the kids to come back from the beach to have lunch. The afternoon flowed leisurely on. We took a nap under the pergola, looked at the photos, talked about my painter; at dusk, we took a short walk toward the hills. Marco fixed Elvira's washer. When the kids drove him to the train station, she hugged him as if he were her own, and gave him a bag full of freshly picked apricots for the trip.

We ate alone, the three of us—Pecorino cheese, a zucchini omelette, and red wine—under the pergola; the grandchildren had gone out for a pizza with their friends.

I left them at eleven, and drove slowly home taking the Quiesa mountain road, the finest and longest. When I reached the pass, I made it longer yet by turning toward Stabbiano. I drove up the woody hill and stopped at the topmost curve. I got out of the car and stood there a while, staring at the moonlit sea; I could hear the thunder in the distance.

The wood behind me resounded with the rustlings of the night: the velvety flight of the predators, the wailing of their prey. The dry barking of a fox reached me from the vines below, like a sudden coughing fit.

Only a small part of my soul was inside my body; the rest, large, soft, and flexible, stretched over the silvery surface of the sea, skimmed over the rounded tops of the chestnut trees, dipped, with roots and worms, under last year's dry leaves and into the damp darkness of the earth, wandered along the strip of country between the beach and the hills, looking for Elvira's and David's house.

I knew ours had been a farewell evening, my farewell to the unlimited breadth of everything, to the possibility of choosing, of changing. In my fifties, I was like Peter Pan, about to fly back through his window to slip into bed.

I am now climbing the steps to my tower: it is one o'clock. The telephone starts ringing even before I can open the door to my bedroom.

"I've been looking for you all day . . . where on earth . . . Oh, Aldo, you're back at last!"

"Lavinia, what is it? What's going on?"

"Nothing, I've missed you. . . . Come down and have a drink with me."

"R . . . right now?" I was about to say "right over." Out of habit—not the habit of answering to such a call, but of dreaming of it: waking up with a pounding heart and lying in bed motionless, trying to prolong that instant of delight and slide back into sleep, into a dream which, instead, keeps receding, farther and farther away from the darkness, into the light of day. Because this time I have no doubts as to the meaning of Lavinia's call: it is the one I've been expecting all my life. But then, how can I explain the fact that I'm not rushing to her side? That I'm not swooping down from my tower window, a solitary crow no longer, but a romantic hawk answering the call of a sweet turtledove? That I carefully turn off all the lights and even find the time to spray my bedroom so that I won't find it full of mosquitoes when I come back?

And, why is it that, as I grab a bottle of champagne from the fridge and walk down to the Limonaia at a fairly swift pace, I feel empty inside, oddly nostalgic, as if I were about to leave a beloved place forever?

I find her on the patio. We open the champagne and symbolically taste it; then we leave the glasses on the stone table and walk away so as not to wake up Nicola.

Our steps lead us toward Villa Grande along the same path we followed the night before. The twenty-four hours that have gone by now seem like an insurmountable caesura. Even the weather has changed: summer, which officially began only yesterday, is already showing the first signs of its end. The thunder rumbles on in the distance, from the gorges of the Alpi Apuane. Over her jeans, Lavinia is wearing a sweater that exudes a faint smell of camphor.

This time she is the one who stops under the jasmine bower. Aside from the thunder and the cooler air, everything is like last night—stars, nightingales, the scent of flowers. But then why does everything seem so different?

"This is the spot where, last night, you took my hand," Lavinia says. Her voice is still quite childish: in the semidarkness, the slender figure by my side could be that of the young girl I met so many years ago. If it is true that a head must have certain requisites to wear a crown, then I am sure hers does not possess them. Just as I am sure that she is not even aware that there is a kingdom to inherit, a kingdom that won't be hers. If she knew it, she would only feel relief.

I wonder whether I should tell Violante that she has made a mistake in her choice of an heir.

"Cynthia and Leopoldo are leaving tomorrow," I say.

"I know. She came to bring Nicola the chemicals to test the water of the swimming pool. Why were you gone so long? Were you angry at me?"

I hold her hands in mine. "No, I was not angry." It will be interesting to see the style of Cynthia's reign. It will certainly be quite different from Violante's. "You know I forgive you everything."

The jasmine gives off a very sweet perfume. I kiss the tips of her fingers and hug her. "Lavinia," I say.

"Yes."

I know I will have to give up something for good. It is like when I see a plane fly very high into the sun: seen from the earth, in the rarefied limpidity of the air, that spot could be paradise. And yet that is not at all the sensation I have when I am on a plane.

I hug her tight. "You have no idea how unhappy I was all day," she murmurs. "I thought I had lost you." She puts her arms around my neck. "You are so tall. The right height for me."

Logically, we would live at the Arnolfina so that Nicola could settle at the Limonaia as soon as he comes back from America for good. And we might want to keep the apartment in Milan. . . .

"I love you, you know," I tell her.

"The funniest thing is that I love you too."

In any case, we are in no hurry. Nicola must spend three more years in America: if we decide to stay at the Limonaia we will just have to make some room for him for two months, during the holidays. . . . Suddenly I feel I couldn't go on living at the Arnolfina. It wouldn't make any sense.

Something is slowing me down, almost paralyzing me. I am suddenly asked to abandon my observatory and step onto the stage. My hands, heavy and awkward as in a dream, move with difficulty as they stroke her supple back. "I can't believe it," I say. Of course, we are in no hurry. A few large drops of luke-warm water are starting to fall from the sky. First we have to wait for the book on Martin Lansquenet to come out. A wave of happiness invades me at the mere thought of the bluish green bird I discovered, of the work ahead, of the book that will be published, of the excitement while waiting for the reviews . . . "I've loved you for such a long time."

Here I am, right at center stage, with the garden and the three houses as a backdrop. Nicola is sleeping in his bed. Violante is organizing her death without knowing that she needn't worry about a thing since everything has already been happily de-cided. Nives is ready to offer her loyalty to the new queen. Cynthia is about to leave on her second honeymoon, but when the day comes she will be ready to dust all the cobwebs off this old kingdom, spray it with a disinfectant, and give it a few fake *settecento* touches; in other words, to do her best, as is her nature. She will have her own personal style, but like Violante, she will behave as if, any moment, she might have to stow all her precious things on an ark, to keep them safe till after the deluge. Marco is traveling south carrying—along with the memory of a strange family—the bag of apricots Elvira Levi gave him—the only thing he has brought back from this trip, his only reward for having set everything straight.

And Lavinia is in my arms. My hands wander up to her hair, so soft. It is starting to rain. Summer seems to have ended; soon we'll move into a very mellow winter, during which we'll decide on lots of things.

Then, we'll see.

FRANCESCA DURANTI's first novel, *The House on Moon Lake*, was a stunning literary debut, winning the Bagutta Prize, the Martina Franca Prize, and the City of Milan Prize. It was translated into many languages. Ms. Duranti has a law degree from the University of Pisa, and has translated novels from French, German and English. She lives in Milan, Italy.

ANNAPAOLA CANCOGNI is a journalist and translator. She lives in New York City.